Chocolate Brownie Genius

by Deborah Sherman

Fitzhenry & Whiteside

www.fitzhenry.ca   godwit@fitzhenry.ca

10 9 8 7 6 5 4 3 2 1

Library and Archives Canada Cataloguing in Publication

Sherman, Deborah (Deborah Faye)
The Triple chocolate brownie genius / Deborah Sherman.
ISBN-13: 978-1-55455-035-7   ISBN-10: 1-55455-035-1
I. Title.
PS8637.H475T75 2007   jC813'.6   C2007-906867-4

**U.S. Publisher Cataloging-in-Publication Data
(Library of Congress Standards)**

Sherman, Deborah.
The Triple chocolate brownie genius / Deborah Sherman.
[192] p. : cm.
Summary: Michael's days as a happy underachiever are over when
he accidentally eats a nanochip loaded with information and becomes
his own worst nightmare: a know-it-all.
ISBN-13: 978-1-55455-035-7   ISBN-10: 1-55455-035-1
1. Science fiction. I. Title.
[Fic] dc22   PZ7.S547 2007

Fitzhenry & Whiteside acknowledges with thanks the Canada Council for the Arts, and the
Ontario Arts Council for their support of our publishing program. We acknowledge the
financial support of the Government of Canada through the Book Publishing Industry
Development Program (BPIDP) for our publishing activities.

 Canada Council   Conseil des Arts
for the Arts   du Canada

Design by Fortunato Design Inc.

Printed in Canada

To Mary and my family.
Thank you for your help
and support.

Prologue

TRIPLE CHOCOLATE BROWNIE DELIGHT. The cause of all of my problems. Would an apple have made me the most hated guy at J.R. Wilcott Middle School? I doubt it. Would a muffin have put me in danger of being the first impeached school president? No way. A slice of pie, an orange, or even a butterscotch chocolate vanilla swirl pudding would have worked. Anything but triple chocolate brownies. With one bite, my life as the most popular president of J.R. Wilcott was over.

I could have eaten anything that day. A cheese sandwich with tomato and mayo. Maybe a handful of M&M's. But when I got home from school that day, all I could smell was chocolate. I had to act fast. Howard was a big-mouth in more ways than one. My little brother had been known to devour a whole pan of brownie delight in one giant mouthful.

Not this time.

I checked my watch: I needed to work fast. I had about ten minutes before Howard would walk through the door. I grabbed a fork and dug in.

Awesome! My taste buds worked in harmony with the chocolate. There was no looking back now. I shoveled it in by the mouthful. I barely chewed; instead I let the dessert slide down my throat. I finished the whole pan in less than three minutes. A new record! My stomach was starting to ache, but it was worth it. Triple chocolate brownies—who knew that my favorite dessert would cause so many problems?

CHAPTER ONE

Hil's Idea

HIL PICKED ME UP FOR SCHOOL every morning at 8:15 a.m. Hilary Rotenberg and I have been neighbors forever. We make a good team. She thinks I'm smart but lazy. She's anything but lazy, and sometimes it even rubs off on me. But not often.

Today she picked me up with a strange smile on her face. "The other day Mr. Kagan asked for nominations for school president. I think you should run."

"Huh?" I said, surprised.

Being school president sounded like a lot of work for a back-row guy like me. Anyway, who would vote for me as school president? There was no way *I* would trust me with important school decisions; why would the rest of the school trust me?

"You're the one with the good grades, Hil. You'd make a better president."

Hil shook her head. "I'm more of a behind-the-scenes type. You're the fun one—everyone thinks you're their friend. Jocks, drama club people, chess league players—you treat everyone the same."

"I don't think so." I felt bad disappointing her, but being president of J.R. Wilcott Middle School sounded like too much work.

Hil didn't give up easily. "We'll do it together. I'll run your campaign and help write your speeches."

I wasn't buying the idea until Hil pulled out her secret weapon. "Student council meetings take place twice a month, *during school hours*. Just think, Michael. You'll be able to skip Algebra every other Thursday."

Math was my worst subject in a long line of bad subjects. Missing *that* class was enough to get me on board.

When we reached school, we went directly to Mr. Kagan.

"Good morning, Mr. K," said Hil. "We'd like a presidential nomination form."

Mr. Kagan was thrilled. "Hilary, I think you'd make a fantastic president—so good that I'll even sign the form for you!"

"Actually," clarified Hil, "it's for Michael."

Mr. Kagan stopped smiling. Hil had a great reputation; my reputation was not so great.

But Mr. K was a fair teacher and willing to give

me a chance. "Michael, I assume that you know how much work goes with this position?"

"Uh huh," I fibbed.

"You'll be the voice of the whole school," he reminded me. "There will be speeches to make, reports to fill out, and meetings to lead—not to mention the school play, the Grade Eight Thespian Extravaganza Extraordinaire. Not only will you have to select the play that this year's class will perform, also you'll have to be hands-on with the production. The extravaganza is the highlight of the school year, Michael. A top-notch production requires a lot of time and effort."

I began to rethink this whole school president idea. Did I really want to be responsible for a whole play?

Hil could sense trouble. "Remember Algebra class," she reminded me under her breath. "No numbers every second Thursday."

The secret weapon! "Sign me up, Mr. K!" I almost shouted.

Later Hil explained my campaign to me: nothing. No speeches. No issues. No debates. No campaigning for votes.

"Don't you think I should have a platform?" I asked her. "You know, like things that I stand for or something? Like spirit days or lost puppies?"

She shook her head. "The kids at J.R. Wilcott are sick of spirit days. They're sick of Academic Olympics and think tanks. They're tired of coming in early to work on the school paper and staying late to work on the yearbook. That's why you're going to win. You're lazy and unmotivated. You refuse to fulfill your potential. With you in power, our classmates know they won't have to fulfill their potential either, except to have a good time."

Hil's logic was brilliant. My main competition was the rich brainiac Harold Wormald. Harold was captain of the Mathletes and chairman of the chess club. He wrote a monthly newsletter called *Hooray for History!* that nobody read.

Harold is a billionaire. His mother invented some sort of talking vacuum cleaner that chats to you as you clean. He's totally full of himself and nobody at school really likes him. But because his parents provide the cafeteria with free ice cream every Friday, we all put up with him. He has a few nerdy friends, but he's actually exactly what J.R. Wilcott was *not* looking for in a president.

Hil's awesome slogan—Have Some Fun and Get a C, Vote Michael Wise for Wilcott President—won me the position by a landslide.

If I had been surprised at my election as student council president, my parents' reaction would have to be classified as shocked. Until the election, my only extracurricular activity had been detention.

"Really?" asked my mom. "School president? Are you sure? It sounds like a lot of pressure."

Mom's a pediatrician. It makes her a bit over-protective.

"You? Student council president? Of the entire school?" sputtered my father when I told him. "You?" he repeated again and again. "You couldn't care less about school. Your teachers are always telling us you need to work to your potential, to pay more attention in class, to get involved in school activities. To show any sort of interest. And now you're school president? Some school!" He laughed until his face turned a bizarre shade of purple. Howard went to get him a glass of water.

But whether they believed it or not, I was now J.R. Wilcott's school president.

CHAPTER TWO

Out With the Oatmeal, In With the Crêpes

OVER THE NEXT couple of weeks, I proved myself to be a basically useless leader, although I did manage to get pizza approved for lunch three times a week. But my next big decision was coming up: choosing a play for the Grade Eight Thespian Extravaganza Extraordinaire. I took submissions from other grade eights and narrowed it down to three worthy choices. Most kids just handed in the names of famous plays, but a few adventurous students wrote their own scripts.

On Monday afternoon, I ate that whole pan of brownies.

By Tuesday morning, I was pretty sure I had zeroed in on the cream of the crop. All I had to do was run it past Hil as we walked to school.

Downstairs Mom was preparing the usual batch

of soggy oatmeal for Howard and me. Every morning was the same story: mushy oatmeal. It tasted like dirty socks—or at least what I thought dirty socks might taste like. And every morning, Mom would stand over us and make sure that we ate at least half of our bowls.

Oatmeal, the Meal of Champions was her motto. "It will make you boys big and strong. A bowl a day and you'll grow as tall as your father. If you're lucky, even taller."

My father hid behind his newspaper. The last thing he wanted to do was call attention to himself. He had been subjected to a daily dose of overdone oatmeal for fifteen long years. Sometimes he begged for mercy, assuring Mom that at age forty he was unlikely to grow any taller.

He sipped his coffee, trying not to slurp and catch her attention. She grabbed two large bowls off the shelf. My stomach began to growl, but not because I was hungry for Mom's breakfast.

It was that whole pan of triple chocolate brownies. I must have eaten them too fast yesterday. I wasn't feeling so hot.

Mom dipped her ladle deep into the pot on the stove. My stomach growled even louder. The sun shone in my eyes.

Everything seemed to be happening in slow motion. She lifted the ladle out of the pot. Runny oatmeal oozed off its sides. Then without thinking, I found myself grabbing her arm and leading her to the table.

"Why don't you take a breather today?" I heard myself say. "Every morning you get up early just to make us a healthy breakfast. Well, today is the day that I take care of you."

Howard and my father stared as I propped Mom's legs up on a pillow and handed her a section of the paper. "Take a load off and relax," I said.

The rest was a blur. Three pairs of eyes stared as I ran around the kitchen grabbing ingredients. A splash of club soda, a dollop of milk, one teaspoon of vanilla, a cup of flour. A handful of walnuts and a little bit of apricot jam.

Voilà! Hungarian crêpes, fresh and ready to eat.

Mom's mouth dropped open. Dad was frozen in bewilderment. Howard began to push himself away from the table. I couldn't blame him; the last meal I had whipped up included a ketchup-caramel-pickle dressing.

"Just try a bite before it gets cold," I begged.

Slowly, three knives cut, three forks speared… and, amazingly, three faces broke out into ear-to-ear grins. Delicious! Howard and Dad shoveled in the food, then raced to the stove to get the last crêpe.

"How did you get the pancake so thin?" Mom asked between mouthfuls. "How did you get them to melt in your mouth?"

Finally, after Howard had licked everyone's plate clean, she asked the most important question. "Where did you learn to make such wonderful crêpes?"

"Family Studies class," I lied. I felt bad about lying to them. But to tell the truth, I had no idea when I had learned to make Hungarian crêpes. Yesterday, I had no idea what a crêpe was—unless you were talking about those crinkly streamers people threw around at New Year's.

"Hey, Mikey." Howard only used my nickname when he wanted a special favor. I knew exactly what he was going to ask.

"Okay, okay. If I get up early tomorrow, I'll make breakfast again."

Howard grinned happily. His smile was contagious; I began to feel generous.

"You can even pick, little bro," I offered. "Belgian waffles with homemade whipped cream or eggs Florentine with minced—"

Mom's mouth fell open.

"Uh, Family Studies," I added, trying to sound

casual. "And a few of those late-night cooking shows."

She seemed to buy it. At least she stopped asking questions. Relief washed over me. But I had to wonder.

Where *did* I learn to cook such an awesome breakfast?

———

I was about to tell Hil all about it, but she was all business when she came to pick me up.

"I'm dying to hear what script you picked!"

The creepy crêpe tale would have to wait.

"How does this sound to you—*Cyborg Robots Fight Till the Gruesome Death*," I said. "It's an action-adventure-mystery that ends in a giant mud fight at the fifty-yard line during the Super Bowl halftime show. Sludge wrote it."

Hil nodded. "Sounds great."

"It's way cooler than last year's stink bomb," I said. "I can't remember what that mess was called."

"*Macbeth*," answered Hil.

"Oh, yeah," I laughed. "Can you believe last year's president chose a boring play by some dead guy? What was the name of that guy again?"

"William Shakespeare," said Hil.

"Shakespeare?" I repeated doubtfully. "He was school president last year?"

"Well, it's pretty obvious you didn't do your English assignment again," laughed Hil. "Last year's president was Alex Baker. I heard that he has yet to live down the mess of last year's extravaganza. My sister told me that he ran for freshman president at Cordella High and got only two votes. Everyone knew about *Macbeth*."

As we neared school, Hil changed the topic to our French test. "Did you learn the dialogue?" she asked.

"Do I ever?" I joked. "I'll just wing it like I usually do."

"You know, one of these days you should just try learning the dialogue. You might find out that it takes less effort than trying to avoid the wrath of Madame Parfait. Maybe you'd even figure out that it doesn't completely suck to know a thing or two."

I was used to this talk from Hil. "First it starts with a thing or two, and then in no time, I'm a know-it-all like that rat-fink weasel Harold Wormald. And then you'd have to go shopping for a new best friend."

Rolling her eyes, Hil dug into her backpack and grabbed a bag full of grapes. "Time for a little pre-test sugar boost. You want some?"

"Nah. One of my teeth is really bothering me, especially when I chew. My mom made a batch of her triple chocolate brownies yesterday and I ate them all myself. I think I cracked a tooth on one of them or something."

"Those brownies," laughed Hil. "You get a crazed look on your face when you inhale those things."

"I know. Usually they're awesome. I don't know what was wrong with this batch, but my tooth has been killing me since then."

"Well, be careful with it. I'll see you in French class," said Hil before we parted ways for our lockers.

CHAPTER THREE

Octo-lingual!

"*MICHEL*, I HOPE YOU LEARNED your speech today. No writing it on your shoe this time?" Madame Parfait stared frostily at me.

It was my turn to recite the French dialogue in front of the class. Rocks Mudman had already mumbled his way through it. And Harold Wormald had just finished performing, flawless accent and all. He gave me a superior sneer as he passed by my desk.

Harold Wormald had been sneering and leering ever since I swept the school elections. Usually his two main pals, his "goons" as Hil sarcastically called them, were by his side. Leon, his fellow nerd, could hot-wire a calculator to make it add when it was supposed to subtract. Fletcher was the muscle of the operation. He was well over six feet and weighed two hundred pounds. Harold kept them close by buying them pizza and Coke.

Today Harold's sneers hardly registered compared to Madame Parfait's expression of annoyance. Looking back, I guess I have to admit that reading the dialogue off the tongue of my shoe wasn't such a great idea. Neither was having my pal Sludge hold up a cue card behind Madame's back—especially when he accidentally held it upside down.

"Stand up and present it to us. *Tout de suite*," she commanded.

But by now my stomach was really burning. My toothache was getting worse, too.

"This dialogue is from lesson four, page thirty-two," I mumbled to the class. I could barely stand up straight. My stomach was cramping and my face began to drip with sweat. The beads trickled down my forehead. I stuck my tongue out to try and cut off the droplets. My mouth felt hot and swollen.

"J.R. Wilcott's fearless leader, unprepared as usual!" Sludge piped up from the back row.

"Go on, *Michel*," encouraged Madame Parfait.

"It's about these people who see a beaver," I whispered. My head was spinning and my hands were shaking. I could barely see straight.

Suddenly, my stomach did an Olympic-sized somersault, followed by two back flips. A bright light flashed in front of my eyes. Then, in a voice not my own— though I swear it came from my mouth—I heard:

"Tiens, il y a castor là-bas!"

The accent was flawless. Madame Parfait nodded appreciatively.

"Ecco c'e un castor di la!" I heard the voice say in expert Italian.

I could feel my lips moving. My Adam's apple bobbed furiously.

"Hej, patrz, tam jest bobr!" the voice continued in Polish.

"Hey Se! Der er en baever derovre!" Now it was speaking Danish!

The class started clapping wildly. Madame Parfait stared at me, speechless. She raised her arms, trying to regain control of the class.

Frantically I looked around. My lips were still moving. I could feel the unfamiliar accents rolling off my tongue.

It was me! It was all coming from me!

I couldn't stop. I recited the line in German, Japanese, Finnish, Gaelic, Mandarin, Czech, Dutch, Swedish, Hebrew, and a local Swahili dialect. The words flowed from my mouth. It was like I was on autopilot. I had no control over my tongue. Portuguese, Hungarian, Russian. The class stood and cheered.

Finally I collapsed in my chair. I was done.

"What on earth was *that*?" Hil asked me after class. "I thought you said you didn't know the dialogue in French. Where did you learn those other languages?"

"I have absolutely no idea. I truly don't. I could feel my lips moving, but I wasn't moving them. And then the words were spewing out of my mouth like a waterfall."

We were sitting in the corner of the cafeteria, eating the pizza my campaign had promised. Kids strolled by, slapped me on the shoulder, and praised my performance in French class.

"Way to shock old Parfait, Mikey!" snickered Sludge.

"How do you say, 'I loved the look on Madame Parfait's face' in German?" asked Genevieve Simon.

Joe Jacobs, the captain of the basketball team, moved in front of Sludge. "Nice job, Mike," he said as he dribbled his basketball. "Have you ever thought about tutoring? I sure could use the help to stay eligible."

Hil sat by as I continued to accept good wishes. Word had spread to the other grades. A table of seveners sent over a complimentary cola.

Finally, it was just the two of us.

I shrugged. "Anyway, as I was saying, I have no idea what happened. It was totally freaky. I swear it wasn't me talking. I mean, I can barely speak

English, let alone Mandarin! All I know is that one second I have a brutal stomachache, and the next second I'm spouting Gaelic!"

"Maybe it was nervous energy," said Hil.

"Whatever. Suddenly it felt like my stomach was on fire. I swear I saw a flash of light right in front of my eyes. All of a sudden I was octo-lingual!"

"Actually, it was more like seventeen-lingual," corrected Hil.

"Whatever," I repeated. "My lips were moving but I wasn't controlling them. I had no control over anything. I swear."

She looked skeptical.

"Come on, Hil!" I cried. "The only Cantonese I know is *sushi*!"

"Actually, that's Japanese, Michael," she replied.

"That just proves my point!"

"You should probably stop falling asleep in front of those midnight cable movies," was Hil's advice. "Maybe the foreign ones are subconsciously seeping into your brain."

"That's all you have to say?" I demanded.

"Well, maybe you should stop having late-night snacks, too."

She wasn't taking this seriously at all.

CHAPTER FOUR

Nano—What?

"MICHAEL, YOU DIDN'T TOUCH your sweet-and-sour chicken," said Mom that night after dinner. My brother and I were helping her do the dishes. Howard scraped and stacked, I rinsed, and Mom put them in the dishwasher.

"Are you feeling okay? The flu is going around school; I had a few kids from Wilcott in the office today. Look at him, Nate. He looks pale."

Dad wasn't paying attention. He was rummaging through drawers, looking behind the counters, and searching under the table and chairs.

Not a day goes by when my father isn't frantically searching for something. Eyeglasses, house keys, car keys, books. Something is always missing. He's a computer programmer, and the house is full of his gadgets. Memory cards, chips, CDs—they're never where he left them.

"Dot, have you seen that new nanochip I brought

24

home last weekend? I'm sure I put it on the kitchen counter."

Mom sighed. "Nate, you always leave chips lying around. Yesterday I put a blue chip in the top drawer of your desk."

"That's not the one I'm looking for," said Dad, shaking his head. "This chip is dark brown. It can store hundreds of gigabytes. It's got three encyclopedias, the complete works of Shakespeare, and full university courses on literature, math, biology, and chemistry on it—not to mention a dozen classic books on world cuisine. A high-capacity removable storage chip like this has never been seen before!"

Howard and I looked at each other. We usually sneak out of the room when Dad goes on about this kind of stuff.

"I could have sworn I left it on the kitchen counter," said my father. "I saw it there Monday morning. I had it loaded up for the shareholders' meeting."

"Well, it wasn't on the counter yesterday when I was baking. You must have put it in a drawer and forgotten which one," said Mom firmly.

I tried sneaking off to my room but Mom caught me. "Do you want something to drink? I can make you a cup of tea and then tuck you in."

Howard snickered behind Mom's back. Sometimes she forgets I'm thirteen.

"I'm fine, Mom. For real. I had a stomachache, but it's almost gone. I just have a bit of a toothache now. That's it."

"It's probably a cavity. You pig out on sweets and then you forget to brush," lectured Mom. "I'll make an appointment with the dentist. Now get to bed and I'll be there in a few minutes."

Sometimes it can be pointless to argue. And my stomach was starting to rumble again. I headed to bed. Mom came in a few minutes later with lemon tea. She sat with me as I slowly sipped the drink.

"Dr. MacIsaac had a cancellation tomorrow at 4:30. I'll come by school to pick you up at 3:30."

Down the hall my father was tearing up the house, still looking for his nanochip. We could hear him pulling drawers off their hinges and dumping the contents on the floor. Soon he was picking through bags of garbage. Then we heard a low sliding noise.

"He's moving the fridge," said Mom. "I'd better go help him." She gave me a kiss and turned off the light. "Get a good night's sleep and you'll feel better tomorrow."

I closed my eyes and tried not to focus on the

fact that it was only 7:30 p.m. Usually whenever I want to fall asleep, I just think of something good, like inventing melt-proof ice cream or scoring the winning goal in the seventh game of the Stanley Cup finals. By the time I get off my wrist shot, I'm dead to the world. I've never actually been awake to see the puck hit the back of the net.

That night I tossed and turned in bed. It was time to rewind the old skating dream.

It was the final game and the arena was overflow-ing with fans. I didn't know if I was going to see any ice time tonight. I had torn my knee up pretty badly the night before...

Another name for the kneecap is the patella, which is the Latin diminutive of the word patina. *Common ailments involving the patella are patellar tendonitis, patellar—*

This was not part of my Stanley Cup dream! Patellar tendonitis? Maybe the toothache was caus-ing me to lose focus. I closed my eyes and refocused on the dream.

The score was 0–0 and time was running out. "Michael, you're on. It's up to you to make something happen," said Coach. "Don't worry, Coach," I told him. "I can do..."

An early name of the Toronto Maple Leafs was the

Toronto St. Patricks. Conn Smythe bought them in 1927 and changed the name to—

Why was all this boring information taking over my favorite hockey dream? It was just like breakfast and French class. This stuff was spilling out of me! It couldn't be just a coincidence. I had to tell Hil all about it tomorrow. Until then, I closed my eyes...

And dreamed about the history of the hockey puck, stick, and Zamboni.

CHAPTER FIVE

Numbers Man!

I FELT A LITTLE BIT BETTER the next day in Algebra class, although I never really felt great when I was dealing with math. We were going over last week's quiz. I got a C minus. Better than I thought I'd do. For a while, my parents made me go to a math tutor, but soon they came to the obvious conclusion that I was not a numbers man.

Mr. Papernick looked around the room to choose someone to go to the board and write the test answers. Harold the Keener sat with his arm up in the air, begging to be called. Mr. Papernick knew better than to pick me, since the object was to find someone with the right answers. I lounged in the back row with Sludge instead.

"I'm totally psyched for the extravaganza this year, man," said Sludge. "Did you get my script approved by Mr. Kagan yet?"

"Tomorrow. I'll present the idea at the council meeting

and see what happens. Don't worry. It's a great play, and Mr. Kagan's pretty cool, for an English teacher. So there should be no problem getting it approved."

With one ear I listened to Sludge brag about his masterpiece; with the other ear I heard Mr. Papernick ask for volunteers.

"Brittany, please go to the board and factor equation number two. Bruce, question number three is all yours." He paused for a moment. "Any volunteers for the bonus question?"

Mr. Papernick always filled his math tests with bonus marks. He said it "encouraged us to try harder." One extra mark for spelling your name correctly. I usually got that one. Two for getting the right date. Sometimes I got that one, too. The bonus question was always the same. According to Mr. Papernick, only two Wilcotters had ever gotten the bonus right—and they went on to be rocket scientists. Hoping to get lucky, we all put down something as an answer. But so far no one had even come close to getting the final bonus question.

Again, Mr. Papernick asked for a volunteer for the bonus question. Sludge slouched down in his seat. No one, not even Harold, volunteered.

My tooth started to ache and my hands felt wet. All of a sudden, numbers started running through my mind. Whole numbers! Fractions! Square roots! A quick flip-flop in my stomach and all of a sudden my mind was racing!

Quadratic equations! The Pythagorean Theorem! Pi!

I could still hear Sludge droning on, "My character will parachute down from the roof of the gym. It might be hard to get Kagan to agree to that, but tell him about the pyro first. Parachuting from the roof will seem pretty tame compared to the fireworks—"

I couldn't hear Sludge anymore. Numbers flashed before my eyes.

My hand shot up in the air. My mouth spoke the words. "I know the answer to the final bonus, Mr. Papernick."

What was I doing?

He eyed me coldly. "You think you can solve the bonus and prove the validity of the Mean Value Theorem? Mr. Wise, you can't even get the date right for two bonus marks."

The rest of the class snickered. Across the room, Hil frowned. She knew something was up. I never raised my hand in class unless it was to go to the bathroom.

"Mr. Papernick, I know the answer to the bonus question. I really do," I told him confidently.

The whole class stopped snickering. They were

all staring at me. Even Sludge stopped rambling and looked on, slack-jawed.

Mr. Papernick frowned. During my whole mathematical career, I had never shown any talent. He held out the chalk to me.

"The floor is yours, Mr. Wise. Prove to us the validity of the Mean Value Theorem."

For a brief moment I wondered what I had gotten myself into. I stood up and felt my legs pushing me toward the board. Along the way, I grabbed the chalk from Mr. Papernick's hand.

I started scribbling as I talked. "Letting $f(b)-f(a) = a$, we can then multiply both sides of the equation by $b-a$. Now, if we get $f(b)-f(a)-a(b-a)$, $f(b)-f(a)-(b-a) = 0$. Let $g(a) = f(b)-f(a)-a(b-a)$. Now then, $g(b) = f(b)-f(b)-a(b-b) = 0$, just as $g(a)$ also equals 0, which is important if we are to use Rolle's Theorem to prove the Mean Value Theorem for derivatives."

I paused to catch my breath and let my scribbles catch up with my explanation.

"Now, instead of using a, we can use x and say that $g(x) = f(b)-f(x)-a(b-x)$ and take its first derivative. According to Rolle's Theorem, since $g(a) = g(b) = 0$, the function $g(x)$ has a value c such that $g(c) = 0 = f(c) = a$ and thus $f(c) = a$.

"Therefore," I concluded, after grabbing a new

piece of chalk, "the Mean Value Theorem for derivatives is proven, and there is at least one value c such that $f(b)-f(a)$ divided by $b-a$ equals $f(c)$."

I finished with a flourish of my hand.

Mr. Papernick looked dazed. The class looked up at him in anticipation. They had no idea if my fifty-three-step answer was totally brilliant or total baloney.

"Enough of Wise's garbage. Let's hear the real answer, Mr. Papernick," demanded a smugly smiling Harold.

Mr. Papernick looked at the sheet in his hand. As he repeated my answer line by line, his eyes began to widen. Sweat seeped from his brow. He spoke more and more slowly, until he finally said the words, "And the final answer is that there is at least one value c such that $f(b)-f(a)$ divided by $b-a$ equals $f(c)$."

Just as I had written! The class broke out into hoots and hollers.

"Way to give it to Wormald," laughed Sludge.

Rocks nodded along with the rest of the back row. "You sure know how to put down that rich geek!"

Harold looked as if he would choke. Leon ran to get him some water. Fletcher encouraged him to breathe into his paper lunch bag.

I walked back to my seat and slumped into my chair, exhausted and embarrassed.

"Mr. P looks delirious. Maybe he'll forget to give us homework," Joe Jacobs said in a low voice.

Finally Mr. Papernick spoke. "Mr. Wise, you have surprised and impressed me no end. In my twenty-plus years of teaching, only a handful of students have solved the final bonus question, and all of those students—"

"Became rocket scientists," finished the rest of the class.

Mr. Papernick continued. "I've always considered you unmotivated and uninterested. But now I realize that all of you have just been unchallenged this whole time! I shall make the next test more difficult. Then you, along with my new star pupil, will feel like you have something more to achieve!"

Sludge shot me a warning look. The cheering suddenly stopped. Did the temperature in the room suddenly drop, or was it just me?

"No, no. P-please, Mr. P-papernick," I stammered. "Don't make the next test harder. This was a fluke. Actually, I hate math. It's boring and pointless. Where would I ever use it in real life?"

"Ah, just as I suspected," nodded Mr. Papernick. "A brilliant but unchallenged student in need of a mountain to climb." He turned to the rest of the class. "In honor of this amazing achievement, I am not only assigning all questions in chapter eight for homework, but all questions in chapters nine, ten, and eleven."

The class gasped. That would take hours!

"Use Mr. Wise as your inspiration. Push yourselves and you'll be amazed at what you can achieve," said Mr. Papernick, smiling.

The bell rang, ending any further mountains to climb because of me.

"Showoff," complained Marty Jenkins as he passed by my desk.

"How do you say 'suck-up' in German?" hissed Genevieve as she stomped by.

Joe Jacobs, who only twenty-four hours earlier had begged me to tutor him, glared at me with the force of a slam dunk. Even Sludge avoided my gaze.

A cold front had definitely moved in.

CHAPTER SIX

Mr. Unpopular

FOR THE SECOND DAY in a row, Hil met me after class with the words, "What on earth was that?" We headed to the cafeteria and settled on a table at the back of the room. I tried to hide behind my books.

"How did you answer that question? Did you look it up on the Net? I know I told you that it was fun to know stuff, but I didn't mean that you should cheat. Did your dad bring home an algebra CD?"

"Hil, you have to believe me. I have no idea how I answered the question. You know how much I hate math. I'm still in detention for another three days for not doing last week's homework."

"Well, there must be some explanation, Michael. I know that you are not as dumb as you like everyone to think. But still, that question was at university level."

"Hil, I mean it! I don't know. I haven't done my homework in ages. Ask me my twelve times table.

I don't even know that. Ask me!" I begged.

"Okay," I continued, desperate to convince her. "Check this out: $12 \times 9 = 108$, $12 \times 10 = 120$, $12 \times 11 = 132$, $12 \times 12 = 144$. See? Those are all wrong. Not even close."

"Those are all right, Michael," she said quietly.

"Well, fool's luck," I said. "I don't know what is going on. Last week, I didn't know those answers. I couldn't speak Spanish or Swedish. I couldn't whip up delicious crêpes in a matter of minutes. And I had no idea that Frank J. Zamboni invented the ice-cleaning machine!"

I was yelling and waving my arms up and down. Kids were starting to stare, so I tried to speak more quietly. "And last week, my mom wouldn't have asked me to cook dinner." I finally stopped my tirade.

Hil looked puzzled. "It's just that the past few days have been so not like you. You sounded like a computer back in math class. And in French class, too—"

We were cut off by a couple of seventh graders. "There's the guy I told you about," the short one said to a taller kid in a striped T-shirt. "Papernick assigned four hours of math homework because of him!"

Out of the corner of my eye, I could see Mr. Papernick striding toward us. There wasn't time to hide under the table.

"Mr. Wise. Just the man I am looking for. I have a proposition for you."

I already knew I wasn't going to like the offer. I just hoped it didn't involve anything that would make the class even angrier at me.

"Your performance in class today was nothing short of astounding," he said. "I don't know if you've heard, but participation on this year's mathlete squad is down. We're barely able to field a full team. Plus, we've had a couple of morale-crushing losses. It's gotten so bad that the team is ashamed to wear their pocket protectors in public." He patted his shirt pocket affectionately. "The mathletes could really use a competitor like you. I think you're just what we need to get out of our funk and bring glory back to mathematics and the J.R. Wilcott Mathlete Squad."

I was horrified. I looked around, hoping no one had heard him. Student council president was one thing. There was something cool about being the leader of your school and getting in pizza three times a week. But there was no dignity in being a mathlete. Mathletes were the worst kind of competitors. Devoted to division, obsessed with equations, fascinated by theorems. Rumor had it that they slept with calculators under their pillows. Joining the mathletes would kill my social life.

Mr. Papernick saw the look on my face. "You're worried about joining the team midseason? Well, there's nothing to be worried about. The team talked it over and they'll welcome you with open arms." He leaned in close. "In fact, between you and me, they're even thinking of making you co-captain with Harold Wormald!"

Hil choked on her chocolate milk. Mr. Papernick stood up to dodge the spray. "Practices are every Tuesday during lunch hour. Bring your calculator and ruler. We'll provide the pocket protector and pencils."

Speechless, we watched him leave the cafeteria.

Then I moaned. "I can't believe it! The mathletes. And co-captain with Harold. I'm going to have to hang out with that rat-fink nerd every Tuesday. Do you think I'll be able to keep this a secret?"

Hil didn't have time to answer. A strange noise in the hallway distracted us. It started off as a low moan. Then it slowly climbed three octaves until it became a high-pitched wail. There was only one thing that could make this noise, and there was only one reason why.

"I don't want to share my captaincy!" cried Harold at full blast. "Especially not with that presidency-stealing, pizza-loving, back-row loser!"

Mr. Papernick ducked his head back into the cafeteria. "Don't worry," he assured us. "Eventually he'll come around to the idea."

Before Hil could make a wisecrack, Mr. Kagan strolled by. "I can't wait to hear your extravaganza choice tomorrow, Michael," he called out cheerfully.

I tried to smile. All I managed was a halfhearted nod.

"Everyone may be mad at you right now," Hil said helpfully. "But once they hear about *Cyborg Robots Fight Till the Gruesome Death*, you'll be back in their good books. Until then, try not to call any more attention to yourself, like solving world hunger or coming up with a cure for the common cold."

She was right. Once people heard about Sludge's play, the four hours of math homework would be forgotten. The bell rang and we headed off to music class.

CHAPTER SEVEN

Saxophone King

HIL AND I HAD NO CHANCE to talk in music class. She sat at the front of the class with the rest of the flutes, while I sat in the middle with the saxophones. Ms. Trilling, our music teacher, had let us choose our own instruments. I'd picked the sax because it looked pretty cool. But it was hard to look cool when I sounded so brutal. I always seemed to be a step behind the music, playing C when it was supposed to be E flat.

I had begged everyone in class to trade instruments with me.

Sludge refused to switch his tuba with me.

"Forget it," said Marty Jenkins, beating his drum.

"Sorry, but I can't play woodwinds. I have a problem with my nasal cavity," said Andrea Hackenpack as she crashed her cymbals together.

I was stuck with the sax.

A first-year teacher, Ms. Trilling was always full of new ideas. We easily agreed with most of her suggestions. Who really cared if we played a waltz instead of a march?

Today, she bounced into the room.

"I can't wait to share this fantastic idea with you," she chirped.

The class shot looks at each other. A teacher with a *fantastic* idea was usually bad news.

Ms. Trilling continued. "Being new to the school, I have a fresh pair of eyes. It's easier to notice things. One troubling thing at J.R. Wilcott is the lack of school spirit, especially at sporting events. Did you know only six people showed up to cheer at last week's volleyball game?"

No one said anything. We were all wondering where she was going with this.

"I spoke to Principal Losman last week, and we came up with a great idea..." She paused for effect.

"Bring back the school band!"

Ms. Trilling waited for the cheers. All she got was a huge groan. Sludge mumbled into his tuba, sending a deep, vibrating rumble around the room.

Ms. Trilling tried to sell the idea. "Our band will be able to play at all the basketball and volleyball games. And maybe even the mathletic competitions. It will be loads of fun. The whole school will come out to watch and cheer with you!"

Nobody moved.

She tried a different approach. "You'll only have to learn three new songs."

It was time to show some of the leadership that had won me the school presidency. I stood up.

"Uh, Ms. Trilling? It sounds like a great idea. Really, it does." A bit of sucking up was a good way to start. "But we're already pretty busy right now. We have to start rehearsals for the Grade Eight Thespian Extravaganza Extraordinaire."

From behind his tuba Sludge gave me a supportive wink.

"We really want this year's play to be awesome, so it's going to take a lot of work. We won't have time to play at basketball games, especially if we want to sound any good." I played a few out-of-tune notes on my sax to back up my point.

"Maybe the grade sevens can do it," piped up Hil.

Ms. Trilling thought it over for a moment. "Well, I suppose my sevens would be able to learn the cheers. They are quite a talented bunch."

We waited for her to let us off the hook.

"I'll make up my mind by the end of class," she finally said. "Now, take out the music for Waltz in A Minor and let's get to work. Marty, I want you to give us a three-beat lead-in. Johnny, you can handle the first solo. And Michael, you take the second."

Was she punishing me for my little speech? Ms. Trilling smiled encouragingly. I decided to try my best not to mess up the waltz.

She picked up her baton and counted the beat. Marty led with his drum solo and we all joined in. We sounded worse than usual. Sludge's tuba was completely off the beat and even Hil's flute was slightly off-key. Ms. Trilling looked discouraged.

Johnny's solo didn't help matters. I felt bad seeing Ms. Trilling's sad expression. On the other hand, our performance meant her talented sevens would get band duty.

It was time for my solo. At this point, I couldn't make things much worse. The rest of the class stopped playing. My first note was A. All I could come up with was B flat. C became D. E became F. My fingers felt heavy and slow. I was already two beats behind the music.

Suddenly, I felt a flip-flop in my stomach.

I saw a flash of light.

My fingers became light and feathery. My touch became easy and effortless. I hit all the right notes with perfect timing. The sound coming out of my sax was smooth and silky.

Ms. Trilling looked up in amazement. I continued my solo with a breezy easiness. She began to tap her foot and move her baton with energy. A broad smile broke out on her face. My solo was over but I continued to play.

The rest of the class put down their instruments.

I played on, cleanly and crisply. Finally, I finished with a burst of staccatos. Ms. Trilling applauded wildly. One or two of my classmates joined in but most of them sat there silently and looked confused.

"Incredible! Incredible!" repeated a joyful Ms. Trilling.

"Showoff," mumbled Marty Jenkins.

The bell rang and we began to pack up our instruments.

"Hey, Ms. Trilling, what about the band?" called out Sludge. "You said you'd make up your mind by the end of class."

"Yeah, remember those talented grade sevens?" Marty added.

Ms. Trilling was still smiling. "None of my sevens can play like that! I'll see you all at band practice next Wednesday at lunch hour!"

I tried to hide behind my saxophone, but that didn't stop the glares. Kids walked by and shook their heads at me. The horn section waved their trumpets and trombones angrily in my direction. For the third time in one day, Marty Jenkins called me a showoff.

At least school was over and I couldn't get into any more trouble.

Hil joined me as I grabbed my coat from my locker. "Maybe I should come over tonight so we can talk about this," she said.

"Why don't you come for dinner? I'm making mushroom risotto and a light melon sorbet for dessert."

She frowned. "What?"

"We eat at 6:30," I told her as I went out to meet my mom.

CHAPTER EIGHT

Nano Nightmare

"ALL THIS TIME WE HAD a gourmet chef right under our own roof," said Mom.

I had just served the risotto. Howard spent the last hour demanding macaroni and cheese, but everyone else was excited to try my creation. I watched closely as they took their first bite and waited for their reactions.

"Awesome!" said Hil. Everyone agreed, except Howard, who was making a fort out of his risotto.

After dinner, I brought out the sorbet. "It should be chilled, but not icy. What do you guys think?"

Everyone had a turn.

"Perfect!"

"Zesty!"

"Tangy!"

Dad was the first to finish his bowl. He wiped the corners of his mouth and leaned back in his chair. "So, have the two of you finally chosen what we'll be seeing for this year's Grade Eight Thespian Extravaganza Extraordinaire?" he asked.

I told him how we had narrowed down the choices to one amazing script and just needed Mr. Kagan's approval.

"And do you mind telling me what the name of this soon-to-be-famous, award-winning production is?" he asked.

Hil and I said it together proudly. *"Cyborg Robots Fight Till the Gruesome Death!"*

He laughed. "Very funny! Now, really. Tell me what you kids have selected."

"Cyborg Robots Fight Till the Gruesome Death is the play we selected," insisted Hil.

"Yeah, Dad. It's a high-speed action-adventure-mystery that ends with a mud fight on the fifty-yard line at the Super Bowl," I added. "Sludge wrote it."

He still looked incredulous. He ate three more bowls of sorbet before we finally convinced him that it was true.

"Can you believe this, Dot?" he boomed. "The world is full of great literary works. George Bernard Shaw, William Shakespeare, Oscar Wilde. And what do they choose? A cheap, chop 'em, sock 'em adventure written by the school thug."

"Hey!" I cried. "Sludge isn't that bad. He's barely been in detention at all this year."

"I can just see it now," Dad continued. "Kids running around the stage, breaking chairs over each other's heads, throwing punches—explosions everywhere."

I didn't see what was so wrong with this picture.

"I wish I could find that missing nanochip," he added. "I loaded it with classic works from great authors." He shook his head. *The Importance of Being Earnest, Death of a Salesman, Hamlet,* and my personal favorite, *Macbeth.*

"This chip is spectacular. Full of so much valuable knowledge. Not only did I download classic plays but, also music lessons for twenty instruments. Flute, tuba, sax… And there was a huge math component through university level. Lessons from great cooking schools all over the world. And the languages on this chip—French, Spanish, Polish, and Czech. I even loaded a local Swahili dialect!"

I looked at Hil. Her mouth was wide open. Gravely she asked, "Mr. Wise, do you have any idea where that nanochip is?"

"No idea. I've been through the whole house from top to bottom trying to find it. I'm sure I put it on the kitchen counter, beside the flour jar. But now it's gone."

"How many times have I told you not to leave your gadgets on the kitchen counter?" said Mom. "It's probably at the bottom of the flour jar. If you'd listen to me, you wouldn't always have these problems."

Hil and I had heard enough. We excused ourselves from the table and raced out to the porch.

"When did you eat those brownies?" she demanded breathlessly.

"Monday, after school. They were fresh out of the oven."

"And when did your dad last see the chip?"

"Monday morning."

"Math, music, cooking, French. It was all on the chip," she said.

I groaned. "And now I'm a mathematical musician who speaks French and Swahili."

"Michael, that chip got into your mom's brownies and now it's in you. You ate it!"

I knew she was right. But hearing Hil say it out loud sent me into a panic.

"My life is ruined because of this! Ruined! I can't have a computer chip in my stomach. I can't be a genius! The whole school hates me! What am I going to do?" I moaned.

For once, Hil didn't have any ideas. "Whatever

you do, try to keep your mouth shut during tomorrow's student council meeting. You don't want to blow it and become the first president of J.R. Wilcott to be axed."

The thought kept me up for the rest of the night.

CHAPTER NINE

Mouth Shut!

USUALLY I LOVE student council meetings—anything to get out of class. But today all I could think about was Hil's warning—keep my mouth shut.

Not knowing what I was going to say or do next was starting to take its toll. To Howard's disgust I burned the Belgian waffles at breakfast. We were stuck eating mushy oatmeal. Later in French class, I tripped on the way to my desk. I could have sworn Marty Jenkins stuck his foot out, but I couldn't be sure. And Harold was still not taking the news of the mathletic co-captaincy well. He, Fletcher, and Leon cornered me after math class.

"I'm on to your scheme, Wise," he sneered as the other two nodded in unison.

"I don't know what you're talking about," I replied wearily.

"Your plan to destroy me. First the school presidency. You don't care about school politics," said

Harold, adjusting his glasses. He sounded a lot like my dad. "And now the mathletes. What's next? My spot as *Hooray for History!* editor? My position as assistant director of the Extravaganza Extraordinaire?"

Ugh. I had forgotten that Harold was assistant director of the play. Leon stood to one side of Harold and fidgeted with his bow tie while Fletcher planted himself on the other side and tried to look tough. As a wannabe group of goons, they weren't that effective. But then Harold gave his armload of textbooks to Fletcher and moved in close. Behind his thick glasses his eyes squinted with anger. He removed his retainer to make sure I'd receive the message loud and clear.

"I'll get you before you get me, Wise. I'm the school's top student for a reason and I won't come second to anyone. You'd better watch your back. Usurp my position and I'll make sure you are very, very sorry." He stormed off with Leon and Fletcher in tow.

Though I wasn't exactly sure what *usurp* meant, I got the message: Harold could be dangerous.

I just wanted things back to normal. I wanted to hang out in the back row with Sludge, make the class laugh at my wisecracks, and drive the teachers crazy. I wanted to go back to being J.R. Wilcott's sub-par leader.

Keep your mouth shut. Just keep your mouth shut, I told myself as I took my seat for the council meeting. If I didn't open my mouth, the chip couldn't spit out any information, and I wouldn't get into trouble. Hil waved to me from across the room. Mr. Kagan did a quick roll call and started the meeting.

"Andrea, can you quickly review last week's minutes for us?"

Andrea Hackenpack was student council secretary. The length of her minutes was legendary. She accounted for everything—including what we were wearing and whether we chewed gum when we spoke. Usually we loved her endless notes; they made sure we missed a whole period of Algebra. But today, I was savoring her epic minutes for another more important reason. The more she talked the less I had to talk. And the less I talked the less chance I would lose control and mess things up. I tried to distract myself with happy thoughts: the highlight reel from my Stanley Cup dream.

Andrea was nearing the end of her recap. "Next up is Mrs. Margles with her monthly review of the cafeteria's lunch menu."

Mrs. Margles stood up, armed with pamphlets, charts, and diagrams. She had been pushing vegetables ever since the school approved my three-times-a-week pizza plan. She set up the overhead and drew what looked like a tree on the board.

"Continuing with my vegetable awareness campaign, today we will discuss broccoli. It's recognized as one of the healthiest foods available..." She droned on and on. I stopped listening.

Suddenly she turned to me. "Well, Michael. As you are the one responsible for massive amounts of greasy pizza every week, I'm curious. What do *you* think?"

"About what?" I said carefully.

"About the broccoli casserole idea."

"Uh, well," I mumbled, trying to stall for time.

"You haven't heard a word I've said about the broccoli casserole, have you?" She was frustrated. "Fine, we'll just start again."

Some of the kids smiled, happy to see Lazy Michael back in action. A few kids glared at me, annoyed that we had to hear more about green vegetables.

Mrs. Margles turned on the overhead again. "What can you tell me about broccoli, Michael?"

I was all set to say *nothing* when it happened.

I opened my mouth.

The words tumbled out. "Studies suggest that broccoli can help prevent breast, lung, and other cancers, as well as reduce the severity of cancers that do form."

"Not again!" cried Marty Jenkins.

There wasn't anything I could do except listen to myself. "Broccoli extract is a rich source of fiber, beta-carotene, vitamin C, vitamin K, and carotenoids. It can play a role in maintaining overall health and promote longevity."

Mrs. Margles tried to break into my speech, but I couldn't stop. "Recent studies have found that broccoli seeds are especially rich in anticarcinogenic compounds. A 1997 study on the antitoxic properties of six polyphenol compounds in broccoli found that most were highly effective at preventing free radical damage to fats."

Mrs. Margles stared. The rest of the class looked disgusted.

"Isn't that...um...great news about the...uh, broccoli?" I stammered, trying to appear casual.

"Well, I can see that you have thoroughly researched the subject," said Mrs. Margles happily.

"Broccoli... What a vegetable," was all I could offer.

"Tell me. Have you also researched the nutritional value of a slice of pizza?" she asked me.

It was like I didn't have a choice: she asked a question and I was forced to spit out an answer.

"A small slice of pizza contains 380 calories, with 80 calories of that being pure fat."

Mrs. Margles nodded. "Did you know that on average most of our students eat two medium slices of pizza for lunch?" She paused and then went straight for the kill. "How much unhealthy, artery-clogging fat would that make, Michael?"

"Here we go again," groaned Marty.

What could I do? "A whopping 160 calories," I answered sadly.

"One hundred. And sixty," she repeated for effect.

I was scared to look at my fellow council members. All I wanted to do was crawl under my chair and disappear.

"What thorough research you have done, Michael," she repeated. "I'm surprised but thrilled. I was thinking about cutting out one day of pizza and substituting broccoli casserole, but your speech reminded me of all the benefits the vegetable offers. Now I'm thinking that we'll change the second day of pizza for a new dish that I've been working on: a broccoli meatloaf mix called *broccoloaf*. I'm sure that Principal Losman will also be impressed and approve my plan immediately."

It was settled. Monday's pizza became broccoli

casserole. Wednesday's slices became broccoloaf. I was going to pay heavily for that one.

"You're a true leader, Michael," she gushed. "Other kids would be worried about what their friends and peers might say. But you're willing to take the brunt of the students' wrath to ensure their health. It takes a strong person to be so bold. They might not thank you now; but they will in thirty years when they're all still lean, mean, fighting machines."

It was hard to breathe. My throat felt as if it were stuck on a golf ball. Judging by the angry faces around me, I might not be around in thirty years. Those "lean, mean, fighting machines" looked furious.

Mr. Kagan called for a five-minute break and Hil rushed over.

"Well, your Stanley Cup dream is not working," she said. "I have an idea. Relax so much that you put your body to sleep. Try and trick the chip into thinking that you are sleeping."

It was worth a shot. Andrea called the meeting to order and we started the committee reports. I concentrated on trying to relax my body. I let my eyelids droop until they almost met. All I could see were the tips of everyone's shoes. I let my muscles go slack. My arms hung limply by my sides and my chin rested on my chest. Drool began to seep down the left corner of my mouth. I felt as if I was in English class, nodding off to the sound of Shakespeare. I couldn't get any more relaxed without falling asleep. Time floated by.

"Thanks to all the committees for such detailed reports," said Mr. Kagan. He turned to me. "Now for our school president. I'm sure you know how excited we are to hear which play you have nominated for this year's Grade Eight Thespian Extravaganza Extraordinaire. Please, don't keep us in suspense any longer."

The whole room turned to me in anticipation. The resentment of the past few days seemed to disappear. They all eagerly waited to hear my announcement.

Just stay relaxed, I told myself. "After…care…ful…con…sider…ation…I…chose…a…play…that…Sludge…wrote…*Cyborg…Robots…Fight…Till…the…Gruesome…Death*," I mumbled slowly, trying to avoid any sudden movements. It was very hard to talk without moving my lips. Because my eyes were still slats I couldn't see their reactions. But I could hear their silence. They didn't like the play I'd chosen?

Mr. Kagan broke the silence. "I'm sorry but I think we all missed that. Could you repeat the name of the play, Michael?"

I repeated the name with somewhat better success.

"*Cyanide Rodents Fly to Great Depths*? What does that mean?" said someone.

"*Silent Rowboats Find Two Grooms Dead*? It's a mystery?" asked someone else.

Realizing I had no choice, I lifted my head gently from my chin. Carefully I opened my mouth. "The play I chose is called *Cyborg Robots Fight Till the Gruesome Death*. It's an action-adventure-mystery that climaxes with a mud fight on the fifty-yard line of the Super Bowl."

The room erupted and everyone started talking at once. They were all smiling. I was in the clear!

"So much better than last year's play," enthused Andrea.

"I totally want to play the part of the most vicious, blood-splattering cyborg," interrupted Albert Hogan, school treasurer.

Everyone seemed to be thrilled with my choice except Mr. Kagan. He looked puzzled and disappointed. We were all still bubbling when he finally spoke.

"A very interesting choice, Michael," he said, stroking his beard. "But are you sure it will appeal to the audience? Remember, you're doing the play for more than just yourself. You're looking to entertain and challenge your audience."

His eyes scanned the whole class. "To capture

audience interest and imagination, a play needs more than a good action scene. It needs motivation, characterization, and plot development."

I began to get a little hot under the collar. "That's not fair, Mr. Kagan. You haven't even read the manuscript. For your information, cyborg robots don't need any motivation to kill. They're just programmed that way!"

My stomach began to do back flips but I was too worked up to notice. "Everyone wants to stick with the same old boring plays, but I want to try something new."

The rest of the council agreed with me. I was the man again! Fighting for the play was just the thing to get me back in with the rest of J.R. Wilcott. Maybe, after helping direct a few car chases, even Harold would lay off. My stomach was burning, but I was caught up in my own hoopla and couldn't stop now.

"Mr. Kagan, there's no reason why people can't be introduced to something new."

He agreed. "Michael, there is nothing wrong with new. New can be fresh and exciting. But on the other hand, there is a reason why some works are considered classics. Shakespeare, Shaw, Wilde—they're still going strong around the world."

Had Mr. Kagan been talking to my father?

"Let's take William Shakespeare, for example.

Can anyone tell me about him? Tell me, what makes the works of the Bard timeless?"

My shining moment was starting to sound like an English assignment, and my fellow student council members had no intention of answering. All eyes were on me.

Keep your cool, Hil mouthed.

But it was too late. My stomach churned and burned. My head filled with sonnets and stanzas. I struggled to keep my mouth shut, but it was being pried open with words.

"Shluppy, schlaffy, shloof." I tried to clamp my teeth together.

"You'll have to repeat yourself, Michael."

"Scroopy, shlonty, schlopps." I was fighting myself to keep quiet. Everyone was looking at me as if I was crazy.

"I told you he can't handle the job," whispered Albert to Andrea. "He's losing it."

"Try it one more time, Michael," suggested Mr. Kagan. "What makes the work of William Shakespeare timeless?"

There was nothing Hil could do to help. The words came tumbling out like a waterfall. "His themes are so universal they transcend generations and stir audiences of every era. Forbidden love, murder, revenge, war—we can all connect to these themes."

"Yes, yes, yes!" crowed Mr. Kagan. "What else connects Shakespeare to the audience?"

I had no choice but to answer. "He was a master at creating the most vivid characters of the stage. Take *Romeo and Juliet* for example. The story itself is not anything new or different, but the way he wrote it is spectacular. His language is poetic, especially when the characters declare their love for one another. Take act 2, scene 2, when Romeo says, 'But soft! What light through yonder window breaks? It is the east and Juliet is the sun.' Elegant and beautiful."

I slowed down, feeling myself run out of energy. Just in time! The situation looked bad, but the damage wasn't permanent. If I stopped talking now, I could still get Sludge's play approved.

Suddenly, I heard the eight words that sealed my fate. Slowly they dribbled out of my mouth.

"It...doesn't...get...better...than...*Romeo...and Juliet.*"

I tried to take back the words, but they were already spoken, just waiting to be pounced on. And boy, did Mr. Kagan pounce!

"I agree wholeheartedly with you. After your glowing reading, I don't see how this year's extravaganza can be anything but *Romeo and Juliet*."

His tone left no argument. The meeting was over. *Romeo and Juliet* it was. I was too petrified to look around. *Cyborg Robots* was just a memory now. My former friends on council were seething with anger. If looks could kill, Albert had me six feet under. Andrea's eyes shone with hatred. The rest of the council was livid. Jill Cabbott, social chair, 'accidentally' knocked my books off the table. She didn't stop to help me pick them up. Neither did anyone else. Those who weren't glaring at me ignored me.

We all filed out for lunch, but not before Mr. Kagan unknowingly rubbed salt in the wound.

"Michael, I hope to see you at auditions tomorrow. Judging by today, I can't think of anyone who would make a better Romeo."

My punishment was just getting started.

CHAPTER TEN

The Ultimatum

HIL AND I APPROACHED the cafeteria cautiously. From down the hallway we could hear everyone yelling. We knew the topic of conversation.

"Maybe we should eat outside," Hil nervously suggested.

But it was time to face the storm. I could be accused of being lazy, unmotivated, or, according to Marty Jenkins, a showoff. But never a coward. My stomach began to do a back flip, but this time it was because of nerves. Hil looked pretty anxious, too. We pushed through the double doors and the roar suddenly stopped.

Maybe this won't be so bad, I thought…

…until I heard the booing and hissing.

"Benedict Arnold," yelled the history club.

"A disgrace to all who wear pocket protectors," huffed the mathletes.

"T. R. A. I. T. O. R!" cheered the pep squad.

Someone threw a piece of broccoli at my head. I ducked.

This was not going well.

The booing seemed to go on forever. I thought about trying to calm the angry mob down and explain myself, but what could I really say? That *Cyborg Robots Fight Till the Gruesome Death* became *Romeo and Juliet* because I had eaten a computer-chip-laced brownie? My schoolmates thought I was a traitor. I didn't need them thinking I was crazy, too.

Suddenly, Harold was standing on top of a lunch table. The threats quickly died down as he called for everyone's attention. He waited until everyone was silent.

I knew that Harold was going for the kill.

"We're all tired of your antics, Wise," sneered Harold. "Your campaign for presidency was one giant lie. Not only have you gone back on all your promises to the student body but now you've got us eating broccoli and performing Shakespeare. According to the *J.R. Wilcott Student Body Code of Ethics*, which I have in my hand here, it's grounds for impeachment. But," he turned and smiled sweetly to the rest of the school, "I believe that everyone deserves a second chance. My generous nature and my position as first runner-up for the school presidency lead me to suggest that you be given one more chance. The Grade Eight Thespian Extravaganza Extraordinaire is the last major event of the school year. But one more extra-credit book report and I'll make sure you go down in history as the first J.R. Wilcott Middle School president to not finish his term!" He slammed his foot down on the table as forcefully as his seventy pounds allowed. His smile was so big that his retainer glistened in the cafeteria lights. Albert Hogan explained to Rocks Mudman and Smashmouth Garello what 'impeached' meant, and the room broke out in rowdy applause.

At least I still had my presidency...for the time being.

But Harold wasn't finished yet. "By the way, since you picked a play that none of us want to do, the part of Romeo is all yours. Be sure to be on time for your audition since you'll be the only person trying out for the part. The rest of us? We can't wait to see you in those little black tights come show time, Romeo!" The class roared hysterically with approval. Harold high-fived Leon and Fletcher. Now he was done!

Things were getting worse every time I opened my mouth. A month ago, I was the popular president of J.R. Wilcott Middle School; a few days ago, I was the annoying president of J.R. Wilcott Middle School; today I was Romeo. Could it get any worse?

Suddenly, two big hands were pushing Hil and me out of the cafeteria. It was Sludge.

"I had the feeling that Wormald was going to try and pull something like that," he said. "I tried to get here in time to warn you, but Papernick really believes in long detentions.

"You've always been in my corner," he continued, "even when the school wanted to suspend me for filling the grade seven marching band's tubas and trumpets with whipped cream. But I gotta ask, what's up with all of this brainiac stuff? It's not you, man."

Hil and I looked at each other. Should we tell him? Would he understand? There wasn't much to lose at this point. Everyone already thought I was crazy, and worse, a showoff.

"Not here," I told him and led him to the library. We grabbed a table in the corner and told him the whole story, starting with the brownies and ending up with the botched Grade Eight Thespian Extravaganza Extraordinaire. It felt good to share the problem with someone. By the time we finished, lunch had been over for twenty minutes. We were missing history class, but none of us cared. Sludge looked stunned.

"Brownies?" was all he could get out. "Brownies?"

"They're my mom's famous recipe," I offered.

"Unbelievable! Just unbelievable, man!"

"Yeah, they are pretty tasty," I agreed.

"I think he means the story," whispered Hil.

That was all he said. We looked on nervously, sweating out the silence, waiting for him to say something—to call us crazy, liars, or worse.

Finally, he spoke. "That's a wild story, man. Wilder than anything I pulled in summer school. What are we going to do?"

Hil's relief was visible. She leaned back in her chair, exhausted. I unclenched my hands, surprised at how slippery they were.

"We need a plan of action, and fast, dudes," said Sludge. "That was one angry mob, led by that fink Wormald. I don't know how long we can hold them off."

He was right. It was time to stop focusing on the problem and start working on a solution. But before we could make any headway, Mrs. Krishnan, the librarian, stepped in front of us.

"I'm not surprised to find you here, Michael. Nor you, Arthur—though I wasn't sure if you knew where the library was," she added sternly. "But Hilary. Skipping class? I hope you are not being led astray by these two unsavory characters."

I apologized to Mrs. Krishnan, explaining that

we'd lost track of time. Sludge promised her he would show Hil the way to detention. At least it would give us a quiet place to make a plan.

The detention room was full of the usual suspects. Jimmy Cuffs, three weeks for letting the school mascot, Gerry the Gerbil, loose; Stan "Fists of Iron" Colla, one week for eating the school's supply of chalk; Allison Applewhite, one day at a time for lateness; Rocks Mudman and Bob Kelly, detained indefinitely for various infractions. Today's supervisor, Ms. Pemberley, didn't care what the offenders did to pass the time, as long as they were quiet. Since the gang was usually the same every day, detention had taken on a family atmosphere. Jimmy Cuffs immediately asked about the health of Stan's Persian cat, which had swallowed a bottle of Liquid Paper the day before. Rocks and Allison chatted quietly. In the far corner sat Bob with a tattered copy of *Romeo and Juliet* hidden behind the pages of a comic book. Hil, Sludge, and I chose the opposite corner for privacy. Hil didn't waste any time.

"I've been thinking," she started. "What we have to do is somehow deactivate the chip before you become the first impeached president in the history of J.R. Wilcott Middle School."

Just thinking about the dishonor made me sweat.

"I think I have a pretty good idea how to deactivate it," chomped Sludge, his mouth overflowing with cookies. "It's pretty simple. You know how a computer loses all function when it short-circuits? Well, we just have to short-circuit Mike."

"Like a giant system crash?" asked Hil.

Sludge nodded. "A computer needs an operating system to function. The operating system runs the chip and allows it to communicate its orders. This chip, it's using Mike's body as the operating system. If we crash the operating system—Mike's body—the chip becomes useless."

Hil looked surprised. The idea actually sounded like it could work. I thought it was brilliant.

"What else would you expect from the creator of *Cyborg Robots Fight Till the Gruesome Death*?" beamed Sludge.

"So, how exactly do we go about crashing me?" I asked.

It was a good question. But Sludge was ready with an answer. "Burn out."

I had no idea what he meant, but I nodded along with Hil.

"A computer needs power to run—energy. With no power, a computer is useless. When you wake up in the morning you have energy. You use this energy through-out the day. You walk, talk, screw up the extra-vaganza—Just kidding, pal," he added when I glared at him. "And the end of the day, you're out of energy. You hit the sheets to power up for the next day."

"What are you trying to say, Sludge?" I didn't understand.

"Basically, Mikey, you're going to have to stay up as long as you can until you have no energy left. With no power your body—the chip's operating sys-tem—will crash and destroy the chip."

Oh.

"There's no time to lose," said Hil. "Tomorrow's Friday. We can start then. I'll bring over some movies to watch."

"And I'll stay over to help keep you up," offered Sludge.

They seemed pretty confident about the idea. The plan was set: a weekend all-nighter. Actually, not only did the plan sound brilliant, but staying up was something I was good at. There were a million things I could do with those hours I usually wasted sleeping. This month's *Bon Appétit* magazine had a wonderful recipe for a cherry soufflé that needed to be undis-turbed if it was to rise to perfection. The house would be quiet enough at 2:00 a.m. to give it a try.

CHAPTER ELEVEN

O Romeo/All-Nighter

I TRIED TO CONVINCE HIL to go out for the part of Juliet, but she was having none of it.

"I don't do love stories," she said.

"But everyone dies in the end. It's more of an action play than a love story. In fact, I think at least three or four people die."

"Is there kissing involved?"

I nodded. "Maybe one or two kisses."

"Then it's a love story. I don't do love stories." There was no changing her mind, not even if it meant leaving me for weeks in Harold's wormy clutches. I went to the auditions alone.

In the auditorium, Mr. Kagan's face broke out into an ear-to-ear smile when he spotted me.

"I'm so glad to see you, Michael," he enthused. "We're going to have a great extravaganza this year!"

Harold, the assistant director, stood right beside Mr. Kagan. A clipboard had replaced his pocket protector but the sneer was the same. He smiled sweetly at Mr. Kagan.

"I agree, Mr. Kagan. And I can't wait to see Michael in those little black tights."

Ignoring him, I took a seat and watched the try-outs. Most of the kids read some dialogue and hoped to be cast in a good role. A few actor wannabes came with a certain role in mind. At the start of her audition, Genevieve let it be known that she was out for the role of Juliet, and only Juliet. She must have practiced in front of a mirror because her reading was terrific.

"Why is Bob Kelly hiding behind the stage?" wondered Mr. Kagan aloud in the middle of her audition.

By the end of the day, most of the parts were cast. There was a Mercutio, Romeo's best friend; his parents, the Montagues; Juliet's parents, Lord and Lady Capulet; Juliet's nurse; Tybalt, Romeo's sworn enemy; and a priest called Friar Lawrence.

"I'm still not sure that I've found the perfect Benvolio—Romeo's cousin and close friend," said Mr. Kagan. But he seemed satisfied nonetheless. He promised to have the cast list posted on Monday morning.

"He gets it from me!"

We had just finished a scrumptious dinner of bouillabaisse, Rock Cornish hen, and rapini. Dessert was a fresh-fruit flan. It had taken me hours to get the bouillabaisse the right consistency. I thought I might have oversautéed the rapini, but everyone assured me it was perfect. Mom was marveling about the taste of the flan to Hil. "Honestly, all these years I never knew what a talented chef Michael was. He was obviously paying attention all those nights I prepared tasty but nutritionally balanced meals."

Howard was playing with his dessert while my father was doing his best to ignore Sludge.

"Anyone want some tea or hot chocolate?" offered Mom after dinner.

"Actually, Mrs. Wise, do you have any coffee?" asked Sludge.

Howard snickered and my dad rolled his eyes. "Coffee! Typical," he mumbled.

But I knew what Sludge was doing. "I'd like to have a coffee, too, Mom."

"Me, too, Mrs. Wise," added Hil. "With extra caffeine if you have it, please."

My mom looked surprised. I never drank coffee. It tasted like bitter turpentine. She must have thought I was showing off for Sludge. But she filled the coffee maker to the top and grabbed three mugs.

"I'll have a cup, too," tried Howard, but Mom silenced him with a look.

As we waited for the coffee, my father asked about our evening plans. "All-night movies," I told him.

He raised an eyebrow at my mother. "It's okay, Nate," she said. "Michael already asked me about it and I told him it was all right."

Hil sensed my dad's reluctance. "We've rented *Romeo and Juliet* to get some ideas for the extrava-ganza," she said helpfully.

"In between *Hot-wiring for Novices* and *Arson for Fire-Dummies*, no doubt," grouched my father, shooting glances at Sludge. "Dot, I really don't feel comfortable about an all-nighter in our house."

We could feel the evening slipping away...our carefully laid plans disappearing...my presidency at J.R. Wilcott imploding!

Sludge tried some damage control. "Mr. Wise, I know you're not thrilled about me and Mike being friends. I can totally understand where you're com-ing from. I don't have the best track record—looking back on it, setting off a giant stink bomb at last year's graduation ceremony might not have been the best idea—but I want you to know that I would never lead

Mike down the garden path. In fact, our friendship has changed me for the better. My only vices now are a good cup of coffee, a strong mug of double espresso, and the occasional triple latte. In fact, to show you how grateful I am at being invited into your home, I brought you and Mrs. Wise a little present."

From behind his chair, he whipped out a big bag of chocolate-covered coffee beans.

"I thought maybe we could have them with the coffee."

While my father wasn't totally won over, he decided that for the time being, I could do worse than have a friend with a caffeine addiction.

"Just keep the noise level low," he warned.

I nodded, but I was no longer listening. Mom had brought over three mugs of piping-hot coffee. Hil and Sludge got busy adding so much milk and sugar to their mugs that soon their coffees were no more than hot chocolate. I took a moment to smell the rich aroma wafting from my mug. Slowly, I took a sip, savoring the rich, nutty flavor.

"Noisette, medium blend. Always a good choice," I said appreciatively.

My mom looked a bit surprised but said nothing. She was starting to get used to her new, sophisticated son.

Finally, Sludge, Hil, and I excused ourselves and settled in front of the television.

Three movies later, Hil had to go home.

"Remember, Michael, it's very important that you stay up," she said gravely. "Do anything—ANYTHING—to keep from falling asleep. Drink loads of coffee. Eat a ton of sugar. A few days without sleep should do the trick. Whenever you feel sleepy, just tell yourself that your future at J.R. Wilcott is on the line." And with those inspiring words of encouragement, she buttoned up her coat and headed out the door, leaving just me and Sludge to handle the situation.

"Sugar packet?" he offered. "They're awesome when you dump them into a bottle of Coke." It seemed like a disgusting idea, but I grabbed a few packets anyhow. Sludge put in another movie and we hunkered down for the rest of the night.

Making it through the first night wasn't all that hard. The movies were okay and the extra-sugary Coke was surprisingly good. Around 2:00 a.m. I thought I saw someone moving on the front lawn. By that time I was pretty drowsy so I wasn't sure if I could trust my eyes.

But a few minutes later, I could have sworn I saw Harold propped up on Fletcher's shoulders, peering through the window, scribbling furiously in a notebook. I immediately told Sludge. He went outside to search the bushes—quietly so he wouldn't wake my dad—and see what he could find.

"I looked all over, man, but I didn't see that fink Wormald or his loser sidekick. You're probably just tired and seeing things," he reasoned.

He was probably right. My eyes began to close around 5:00 a.m., but a quick-thinking Sludge slung me over his shoulder like a sack of potatoes, carried me upstairs, and threw me into a freezing shower.

"I know this may seem a little rough right now, pal," he said as he turned the cold faucet as far as it would go, "but as Hil said, your future at Wilcott is on the line!" Minutes later I was wide awake—teeth chattering but wide awake. We headed back downstairs to watch the end of the movie and catch the sunrise.

CHAPTER TWELVE

Riding the Wave Fully Loaded

MOM CAME DOWNSTAIRS in her bathrobe at 8:00 a.m. "I can't let our guest eat cold cereal." She smiled. "What'll it be, boys? Omelets? French toast? Pancakes?"

I was feeling sort of drowsy and craving another sugar rush—maybe a hot fudge sundae or a piece of cherry pie a la mode. But French toast could also work.

"French toast would be great," replied Sludge, reading my mind. "And to thank you again for having me over, Mrs. Wise, I wanted to give you another little present." He handed her a massive box of candy. She had to use both arms to cradle it.

"How...ah...generous, Sludge. There must be five pounds of candy here. You *really* shouldn't have."

"It's just a small token of my appreciation," he replied, winking at me.

"Can we open it, Mom? Please?" I begged.

"Isn't it rather early in the morning to be eating candy?"

"It's never too early!" I said, returning Sludge's wink and ripping open the box.

While Mom was whipping up breakfast, I downed fifteen chocolate-covered caramels, nine chocolate-covered cherries, and six truffles. I was ready to throw up.

"One last praline." Sludge pushed the box at me.

"I can't," I moaned. "I think I'm going to be sick."

"You'll need all the sugar you can get to make it through these next few days," he reminded me. "You might not think so now, but in a few hours when you're riding a wave of energy, you'll be thanking me for stuffing you full of sugar."

"But I *really* think I'm going to be sick," I warned desperately.

At that moment, Mom entered with a stack of French toast. She put the platter down in front of us and headed back to the fridge to get the maple syrup.

"You got any icing sugar?" asked Sludge. "It really completes the dish."

I was sure I'd be ill when Mom put three slices of French toast on my plate and handed me the giant bottle of syrup. I lightly drizzled my plate with the sticky stuff.

Soon I was ready to ride that wave of sugary energy by going for a run. We were lacing up our shoes when my dad came downstairs.

"I found this in the bushes when I went to get the paper." He reached into the pocket of his robe and pulled out a piece of familiar yellow plastic. Shaped like a library card, with the initials *H.W.* monogrammed in the upper-left corner, Sludge and I recognized the pocket protector immediately. I hadn't been dreaming last night. It *was* Harold in the bushes spying on us!

"I assume this isn't yours?" Dad asked Sludge, waving the yellow protector in the air. Sludge and I exchanged worried looks. That rat-fink worm was determined to mastermind my downfall and make my life miserable.

"We'd better not underestimate the little fella," said Sludge. "Remember that detention paper I had to do on Napoleon Bonaparte? The short guys are usually the meanest, especially when they think they've been double-crossed."

I hadn't told Sludge and Hil about the threatening note I had found in my locker. It was supposed to be anonymous, but Harold was the only person in school who'd write nasty notes in calligraphy. Spying on me at home was a whole new low for him. Somehow I was going to have to stay out of his way *and* keep an eye on him.

I spent most of Sunday lying on the couch doing the *New York Times* crossword puzzle and watching cooking shows. Hil and Sludge called every hour to make sure I was awake. I was, but barely. I had no energy.

The plan was working.

CHAPTER THIRTEEN

Louisiana's Purchase

BY MONDAY MORNING, I was beat. The chip *had* to be close to crashing; I was about to fall on my face.

At lunch in the cafeteria, Hil nibbled on a cheese sandwich while I munched on a couple of donuts, a few Twinkies, and a latte. In the past three days, I had drunk so much coffee that it was pumping through my veins.

Harold, Leon, and Fletcher walked by, each holding a steaming cup of coffee. Leon and Fletcher were arguing about how to make it taste better.

Hil tried to keep my spirits up and my eyes open. "You've made it through French and English. Just three more periods. We'll test the chip right after class. Either way, you'll be sleeping in a few hours."

Genevieve stopped by our table. *"Bonjour, Michel,"* she purred.

Hil rolled her eyes as far back as they would go.

"Oooh, coffee! My favorite," she cooed, ignoring Hil. "How mature and manly."

"Hi, Genevieve," I replied, trying to sound casual. "How goes it?"

"Well, Michael, I don't know if you've heard yet, but Mr. Kagan posted the cast list and I am your Juliet." She smiled proudly. "We really don't have much rehearsal time, so I thought we could get together as soon as possible and run lines. Ours are the most important scenes in the play. We need to work together to make sure they are *spectacular*."

"Um, okay. When did you have in mind?" I was hoping it wouldn't be today; I needed something to keep me awake. *Romeo and Juliet* wouldn't do the trick.

"After school tomorrow?" she asked. "I'll meet you in the library?"

We agreed and she began to leave. Suddenly she turned around again. "You know, Michael, I am very excited about this. The talk around school is that you've lost it, gone off the deep end, totally cuckoo, a few bricks short of a load, a couple sandwiches short of a picnic. But I still like you. I'll see you after school tomorrow." And with that she turned and flounced away.

Hil decided another pep talk wasn't needed. "Do you need more inspiration than that?" she asked, laughing.

Staying awake through Math wasn't a problem. Mr. Papernick had me up at the board solving advanced quadratic equations. The rest of the class looked bored, but the work kept me focused.

Science was a breeze. I dissected a frog in front of the whole class. Focusing on a specific task was a big help.

I ran into problems during the last period of the day, History. Ms. Pemberley was lecturing from the textbook again. If that wasn't boring enough, the topic was the socioeconomic fallout of the Louisiana Purchase. The subject was drier than the Sahara desert. Unfortunately Hil was in study hall and Sludge was in shop class—I was on my own. Ms. Pemberley's monotone wasn't helping matters.

As she starting droning on about Napoleon Bonaparte's vision of France, my right eye began to twitch. I closed it for some relief, reasoning that my left one would still be open. When my left eye began to twitch, I debated closing it as well. I figured that although both eyes were closed, my ears would still be open. It seemed like a good idea, so I closed both my eyes and began to relax in my seat.

Suddenly, Ms. Pemberley was barking my name. "Michael! I know you've been extending yourself these days with all of your extracurricular activities, but that's no excuse for sleeping in my class."

The rest of the class turned and looked at me proudly. Gingerly, I felt around the corners of my mouth—they were dry. At least I hadn't been drooling.

Ms. Pemberley broke into my thoughts. "Since you find it unnecessary to pay attention, why don't you sum up the socioeconomic effects of the Louisiana Purchase for the rest of us."

Thirty pairs of eyes widened. I knew they were hoping that I wouldn't know the answer, that the man they had voted in as J.R. Wilcott Middle School president—the chronically late, dependably average guy—was back.

Maybe I *was* back. I had no idea what the socioeconomic effects of the Louisiana Purchase were. Not only did I not know the socioeconomic effects, but I also had no idea who Louisiana was and what she had purchased.

It felt so good!

Sure, we might be stuck performing *Romeo and Juliet* at the extravaganza, but everything else could go back to normal. I joyfully prepared to tell Ms. Pemberley I had no idea what she was talking about when I felt the familiar rumbling in my stomach. A familiar flash of light followed, and out it came in a torrent.

"The United States acquired Louisiana from Napoleon Bonaparte's France on April 30, 1803. The land, sold for just $15 million, became thirteen states: Louisiana, Arkansas, Missouri, Iowa, North and South Dakota, Nebraska, Kansas, Wyoming, Minnesota, Oklahoma, Colorado, and Montana. The deal—one of the greatest real-estate deals in history—doubled the size of the U.S. and put the country in a position to become a world power. The deal also greatly strengthened the country materially and strategically, while also providing a powerful impetus for westward expansion."

"I could have sworn you weren't listening," mused Ms. Pemberley. "Nonetheless that answer is absolutely correct."

The whole class looked at me with disappointment. Slowly, each face turned from me in disgust until I was facing thirty hostile backs.

"It's no use," I told Hil after class. "I've been up for over seventy-five hours and, trust me, a system crash is nowhere close to happening."

"I heard what happened in History," she sympathized. "I guess it's about time we give up on this plan and move on to another one. I had a feeling this one might not work, so yesterday Sludge and I brainstormed and came up with half a dozen other ideas. We can head over to his place and go over the list if you like."

"Actually, I think I'm going to head home and go right to bed. The chip may not be ready to crash, but I am."

Chapter Fourteen

Lip-to-Lip Contact

Twenty hours later I woke up to my mom's gentle shaking. Yawning, I glanced at the clock. It was Tuesday. I had slept until noon.

"You looked so tired yesterday that I let you sleep," she explained. "You've got so much on the go these days. You're a little run-down."

I took a quick shower and then went downstairs to prepare a healthy breakfast.

Using a few eggs, fresh tomatoes, mushrooms, and green peppers, I made a huge egg-white omelet, which I cut in two. I put half on a plate for my mom. After I cut up a fresh kiwi and squeezed us some fresh orange juice, we sat down to eat.

"I forgot to tell you," said Mom, in between bites. "A Genevieve called a few minutes ago. She wanted to remind you that you're running lines with her after school."

"She's playing Juliet," I explained to my mom. "She's really psyched about practicing with me for some reason."

Mom just smiled and continued to eat her omelet.

Fourth period was just finishing when I got to school. Hil and Sludge were in their seats. She gave me a thumbs-up. He gave me a wink. I was anxious to hear our next step.

Unfortunately, Mr. Fishbaum was lecturing about the weather patterns of Southern Mongolia. The class was either bored into a stunned silence or dozing quietly—any attempt to whisper would easily be detected. The bell finally rang and I headed over to my friends.

Before I could get there, Genevieve swooped down on me. She was dressed head to toe in black, complete with a black beret on her head. I guess it was her dramatic look.

"O, Romeo!" she trilled, "Romeo, wherefore art thou Romeo? I'm in character right now, and I don't want to lose it," she added in a whisper.

"I guess we have to go practice now?" I asked her. Not everyone had the benefit of a computer chip feeding them their lines. I'd have to catch Hil and Sludge later.

We headed to the library and found a quiet corner.

"Why don't we start with the balcony scene—you know, act 2, scene 2?" I suggested. "It's one of the dramatic high points of the play."

"Actually, I was hoping we could start with the scene where Romeo and Juliet first lay eyes on each other. It's my favorite," said Genevieve slyly.

I shifted uncomfortably. I knew why it was her favorite: there was lip-to-lip contact in that scene. And not just once, but twice! Almost every girl in the whole school hated my guts, and I had to be stuck playing Romeo to the only one who wanted to smooch!

"Um, actually, Genevieve, I haven't learned that scene yet," I lied.

She pouted. "Well, you'd better learn it soon. Rehearsals start next week, and we have a run through in a couple of weeks. We have to have the scene perfected by then."

I shuddered. While the thought of kissing wasn't as revolting as it had once been, I really didn't want my first kiss taking place in front of a sold-out audience of snickering classmates. What if I did it wrong? If I bit her lip or clacked her teeth against mine? Sludge, on the other hand, thought that public kissing was great, up there with hockey and tattooing.

"You're a lucky man," he had told me on the

weekend. "Genevieve is hot, and you get to kiss her. And in front of the whole school!"

"Twice," I had answered, trying to sound enthusiastic. ·

"You'll enjoy it," he had said, slapping me on the back, laughing. "It's almost worth joining the play."

Genevieve and I ran through our scenes—minus the kissing ones—twice. She seemed satisfied that I knew my lines and complimented me on my delivery. She nodded her head enthusiastically during my soliloquies, punctuating each one with "Excellent!" or "Great!" or "So much raw emotion!"

We called it a day after spending a little extra time on the last act. I was packing up my bag, relieved that our rehearsal had gone so well, when she uttered the dreaded words.

"Next Monday we're going to go over all of our scenes for Mr. Kagan. *All* of our scenes. I'll bring the spearmint gum."

I shuddered at the thought.

By the time I arrived home, I had two messages to call Hil. I grabbed an apple and ran to my room to call her back. I started blabbering on about Genevieve and her eager lips, but she cut me off.

"I have it, Mike! I have the answer to your problem! Well, this idea didn't make the list. But that's because I just came up with it. Sludge thinks holding you upside down and shaking the chip out of you is a great idea, but I am positive this idea will work better."

"Tell me," I begged.

"Well, we tried to destroy the chip by crashing your body. But your body didn't crash because we kept providing it with a constant energy source: sugar! The sugar you ate to stay awake actually worked to fuel your body."

So far, it made complete sense.

"What we really need to do is the exact opposite."

Now I was lost. "Huh?"

"A computer, a television, a hair dryer... What do they need to work?"

Energy! I was starting to clue in to Hil's new plan.

"A computer needs energy to work," she continued. "Batteries or an electrical outlet. If we get rid of your body's energy source, the chip will have nothing powering it and won't be able to function. Your misery will be over!"

"You mean food," I said slowly. "If I don't eat any food, I'll deprive the chip of its power source. And with no power, the chip is useless."

"Bingo!"

Hil's logic made sense, although a week earlier, Sludge's "no sleep" logic had made sense, too. I was worried. I was still feeling the effects of the coffee–chocolate–French toast smorgasbord, but how long could I go without eating altogether?

"We'll just take it day by day and see how it goes. I'm hoping that just a few days will do the trick."

I decided not to remind her that she had also "hoped" the last plan would take "just a few days."

"We'll make sure you don't starve," assured Hil. "We can't let our Romeo faint in the middle of the balcony scene, can we? It would ruin the play—not to mention Genevieve's hopes and dreams."

"Very funny," I growled. "Now that we have a plan for the chip, we have to come up with another plan to get me out of kissing her in front of the whole school."

Hil ignored me. "By the way, did you know that Sludge is thinking of understudying the role of Romeo? He says he's only considering it so he can watch your back, but I don't believe him. After all those times he said his dog ate his English homework, who knew that he would actually be hoping for a chance to be in a Shakespearian play?"

CHAPTER FIFTEEN

Practice Makes Perfect

THIS PLAN WASN'T SO DIFFICULT. The trickiest thing was avoiding eating without making Mom worried or Dad suspicious. But with the play right around the corner, I was spending a lot of extra time at school anyway.

Genevieve kept suggesting that we rehearse together, but I had a list of excuses. Most of the time, I told her Bob needed extra work on our scenes. He had secretly auditioned and won the role of Romeo's mortal enemy, Tybalt. We were all shocked to hear that bumbling Bob had made it through auditions without tripping over his giant feet. His permanently undone shoelaces didn't help much. He was a rubbery mess of arms and legs. And he wasn't known for his love of Shakespeare.

"I ran out of hot rod mags and had nothing else to read in detention" was his explanation. "It's a pretty cool story, actually. Lots of death—

though it could use a little more destruction."

Sludge thought the play was cool, too. "It doesn't get better than forbidden love, man! Romeo loves Juliet. Juliet loves Romeo. But a stubborn family feud stands in the way of their true love."

Today we were blocking our scenes—learning where to stand when we were on stage. As the assistant director, Harold positioned us on our spots. Smiling evilly, he kept placing me halfway offstage. For the important balcony scene, he had me standing behind a giant tree.

Mr. Kagan was hoping today would go well and we would be prepared for a full run-through next week.

"Act 1, scene 1!" called Mr. Kagan. Bob gave me the thumbs-up and headed out to the middle of the stage. I listened hard so I wouldn't miss my cue. It was only twenty-four hours into Hil's new plan and I was feeling good. Hunger had yet to set in.

Bob was making it through most of his dialogue, with only a minor stumble here and there. I knew he'd had trouble learning his lines. The last time he'd sat beside me in detention, the frustration was written all over his face.

"I'm trying, man. I really am," he'd said. "But it's hard learning all these words. Especially because I don't know what I'm saying, with all the *thees* and *yonders*. How did you learn all of your lines?"

"Repetition, Bob. Repetition." I'd felt guilty lying to him, but what else could I say? The chip was making it easy to learn my lines. The dialogue was already inside of me. I had read through the play once or twice, just to practice when to lower my voice, when to raise it, and when to pause for effect, but I knew the play inside and out. And, though it was hard to admit that my father was right, *Romeo and Juliet* was a pretty good tale. It was no *Cyborg Robots Fight Till the Gruesome Death*, but I could see what Mr. Kagan meant when he called it a classic. It surprised me to realize I wanted to do a good job as Romeo. Of course, with the chip fully operational, I didn't have much to worry about.

It was my cue. Striding confidently to the middle of the stage, I looked out into the empty auditorium, past Mr. Kagan, and with a flourish of my left arm, shouted clearly, "Good morrow, cousin."

Practice was going well. Rocks Mudman, forced into the play as his only chance to pass English, made a surprisingly good Benvolio, Romeo's best friend. He and Bob frequently ran lines in the back of detention.

"Excellent! Excellent!" cried Mr. Kagan. "Act 1, scene 5."

Ugh. It was time for the dreaded meeting between Romeo and Juliet—well, maybe not dreaded for Romeo and Juliet. And *definitely* not dreaded for Genevieve, who popped a fresh piece of spearmint gum in her mouth and smiled.

I had no intention of kissing Genevieve in front of all of these people today. Quickly I checked the slip of paper where Hil had jotted down a list of excuses for getting out of kissing Genevieve. *Running lines with Bob* was no good; neither was *blame the West Nile Virus*. I didn't even have a clove of garlic handy. Hil's excuses were useless today. I had to think fast.

Walking out to the middle of the stage, I avoided Genevieve's gaze. Looking at my scruffy tennis shoes, I muttered my lines, "My lips, two blushing pilgrims, ready stand to smooth that rough touch with a tender kiss."

Genevieve tried to gaze soulfully into my eyes. "Ay, pilgrim, lips that they must use in prayer." She put her hands on my shoulders, closed her eyes, and leaned in for the big moment.

Quickly I ducked. "Huge fillings," I explained. "Dentist said I shouldn't do anything with my mouth except talk slowly and drink liquids."

Genevieve was furious. "We're supposed to be going through the whole play today!"

"I know, I know," I told her, trying to sound disappointed. "I feel terrible about it, but I have to follow the dentist's orders. I'm sure I'll be able to do the scene by the middle of next week."

"You'd better," she huffed.

I was off the hook and had bought myself a little bit of time, but I was quickly running out of excuses.

CHAPTER SIXTEEN

Roast Beef, Gravy, and Garlic Mashed Potatoes

I HAD A BIG PROBLEM.

For the past few days I had been doing all of the cooking. It was a lot easier to hide my fasting if I was in charge of making the food. Sometimes I lied and said that I had eaten as I made dinner—tasting the soup to make sure it wasn't too watery or sampling the pasta to make sure it was al dente. Other times, I kept jumping up from the table, seeing to it that everyone's plate was full and dessert was being warmed to the perfect temperature. I managed to distract my parents just enough. They never noticed that I was only pushing food around my plate.

But that night Mom decided to surprise me with a special dinner.

"You've been whipping up gourmet feasts for us every night," she smiled. "I wanted you to have a break."

She had planned a meal of my favorites: roast beef, gravy, garlic mashed potatoes—and triple chocolate brownies for dessert! This was going to be rough.

Over the past few hours, the hunger pains had become powerful. I was going to need a lot of support to make it through a roasted, mashed, triple chocolate meal!

"Can I invite Sludge and Hil for dinner?"

I couldn't find my mom so I nervously asked my dad. Luckily he was busy looking for a CD. He managed to mumble a distracted "Whatever."

I called Hil first. "I wish you had called an hour earlier!" she said. "I just agreed to go to the movies with my cousin."

"It's okay," I reassured her. "I'll call Sludge. I'm sure he has nothing better to do, as long as he's not grounded."

I was right. "Just tell me when to be there," said Sludge happily. "My grounding finished yesterday and we're having sardine sandwiches for dinner tonight."

"Hurry!" I begged him. I could already smell the

roast beef cooking in the oven. The aroma was making my stomach rumble.

———

"It smells delicious, Mrs. Wise," Sludge said to my mom.

And it did! We took our seats, Howard to my left and Sludge to my right. He gave me a wink just before Mom brought out the salad. The challenge was on.

Passing on salad was no big deal. Lettuce and celery were never my thing anyhow. But the main course was a different story. Mom brought out dinner dish by dish. She placed the roast beef in front of my father and handed him the serving fork. I was worried she would think I was run-down again if I said I wasn't hungry. So I let my plate get heaped high with food.

Usually I detested peas and carrots, but today even the veggies looked good. Sludge saw me ogling my plate of food. He watched as I licked my lips, imagining the tender meat melting on my tongue. I needed him now more than ever!

"Delicious roast beef, Dot," complimented my dad.

"Actually it's a little tough and chewy," Sludge said to me, his mouth full of roast. My father glared at him.

"Try another piece, Sludge. Something rare?" asked my mother.

Sludge forked a piece of roast beef from the middle. He took a bite. "Actually, this piece is pretty tough, too, Mrs. Wise." He turned to me. "Don't worry, Mike, you're not missing much."

My dad looked furious and Howard tried not to giggle.

For a guy who didn't like his dinner, Sludge was quickly shoveling a lot of food in his mouth. Earlier we had made plans that midway through the meal, we would swap plates. Sludge would whisper "Now," and I would switch our plates. Sludge was quickly trying to clear his plate so I would end up with an empty dish. But our plates were so full that it was impossible for Sludge to clear the mountain of meat and potatoes in front of him.

It was just about time to put the plan into action. Unfortunately, the whole family was staring at Sludge cramming three pieces of roast in his mouth. Somehow I had to distract them.

"Hey, everyone," I said, trying to get their attention.

Their eyes stayed glued on Sludge as he made room in his mouth for a huge helping of potatoes. His cheeks were stuffed and he looked like he might explode.

"Hey, Mom and Dad," I tried again. "The play is going really well."

"Mmm," they replied, still watching Sludge with fascination.

Sludge quickly figured out what the problem was. With a big, long gulp he managed to swallow the three pieces of meat and one and a half potatoes in his mouth. Suddenly, he stood up and pointed across the room.

"Mouse!" he yelled at the top of his lungs. "There's a mouse in the corner! Everyone, take cover!"

My parents were on their feet. Howard ran from the table. Sludge quickly switched our plates.

After spending a few minutes trying to find this mouse, my dad returned to the table.

"I don't know what you saw," he said to Sludge angrily, "but there is no mouse in our home! Maybe if you stopped eating like such a—"

Mom cut him off by changing the subject. "Does everyone like the potatoes? I added fresh garlic."

"Terrific!" "Creamy!" "Delicious!" we replied.

"Too lumpy!"

It was Sludge again. "Way, way too lumpy and not enough salt." He turned to me. "You could do much better than these mashed potatoes."

My father's face was redder than the tomatoes in the salad.

Sludge kept doing his best to convince me the food wasn't worth eating. The gravy was "runny," the carrots were "mushy," and the peas were "too green." But I could see by the way everyone was asking for seconds and thirds that he was lying. I began to seriously consider a forkful of mashed potatoes. How could one bite of mashed potatoes hurt? Potatoes weren't even high in sugar—I remembered Mrs. Margles saying they were a starch. One mouthful of Mom's creamy mashed potatoes couldn't hurt.

Sludge could see it in my eyes that our plan was in jeopardy. Drastic measures were needed! He grabbed my fork of potatoes and put it in his mouth.

"Yum!" he crowed. He took another forkful and another forkful and yet another forkful until my plate was clear of potatoes.

"Delish!" he howled. The rest of the table watched him in wonder.

"For someone who claimed the potatoes were too lumpy, you sure seem to like them," muttered my father.

Sludge moved on to my roast beef. He shoved each piece into his mouth quickly. "These pieces aren't tough at all," he said, gravy dripping down his chin.

Everyone was staring.

Knowing I wasn't a huge vegetable fan, he just

picked at my peas and carrots. Mom went to the kitchen and came back with her triple chocolate brownies. My mouth began to water. Howard ran to the freezer and got the vanilla ice cream.

Brownies a la mode!

Mom cut me a huge brownie. "Your favorite," she said, handing me a big chocolate chunk.

She didn't need to remind me. I tried to resist. I really did. But it was getting harder and harder with every sweet-smelling moment. It didn't help that Howard moaned in ecstasy after every bite. Sludge knew I was in trouble, but after eating six pieces of roast, five helpings of mashed potatoes, an assortment of vegetables, and one huge brownie, he had finally run out of room. Thinking quickly, he grabbed the first thing he saw: the salt shaker.

"I think it could use a little of this," he told me, emptying the shaker onto my pie.

"Now you've made it too salty for him, Sludge," said an exasperated Howard.

"You're right," agreed Sludge. "Maybe some pepper would help."

He grabbed the shaker and turned it over on the brownie. Soon, the chocolaty top was covered in gray flecks. Still, the brownie looked edible. Sludge grabbed the dish of gravy we had forgotten to clear.

He drizzled it over my dessert. If I squinted hard, it almost looked like chocolate sauce! He dug deep into the bowl and came up with an extra lumpy spoonful. He dropped it on the brownie, drowning the delicious, melt-in-your-mouth chocolaty goodness in brown glop.

I was finally defeated. The brownie looked revolting. I pushed the plate away from me.

"There's still one more piece," offered Mom. "Just topped by ice cream this time?"

It was too late: Sludge had grabbed the pan and devoured the last slice.

<hr>

After dinner, Sludge and I cleared the last of the plates. I didn't know how to thank him. He had sacrificed himself for my sake. Not only had he stuffed himself silly, but he had acted like a complete buffoon in front of my whole family. I opened my mouth, but words couldn't express my gratitude. Sludge was a true friend. One of the best I had. He was getting pretty good at reading my mind; he gave me a wink.

"You're welcome," he said.

Chapter Seventeen

The Stomach Rebellion

BY MONDAY MORNING, the gentle growls in my stomach had turned into rowdy rumbles. It felt as if there were an earthquake happening in my belly. I swore I could hear my body talking to me.

Feed me, whispered my stomach.

A bagel will do, murmured my small intestine.

It doesn't even have to be buttered! screeched my esophagus.

My stomach rumbles had become so loud that I barely heard my dad say goodbye as he left for work.

When I got to school I told Sludge and Hil.

"We got it covered," said Hil as we walked into Mr. Thatcher's homeroom class.

As he took attendance, my stomach let loose with an embarrassing roar. It sounded like a jet plane taking off. A few kids turned around to see what the noise was.

Suddenly, there was a big thud. Hil had knocked her pencil case and binder off her desk. The kids turned their attention to her as she picked up her stuff.

I nodded thankfully to her and slumped even further under my desk. Soon the rumbles started again. Everyone could hear them! I could feel my face turning pink with humiliation. Beside me, Sludge started to cough. He continued to cough louder and louder until he sounded like a bullfrog choking on a piece of licorice. But it did the trick. No one paid any attention to me and my empty stomach.

Sludge and Hil spent the rest of Homeroom sneezing, wheezing, and falling off their chairs to distract the class from my rumbling.

The bell rang and we headed to math class. Hil went straight up to Mr. Papernick and had a quiet conversation. He made a beeline for me.

"So, Mr. Wise, Ms. Rotenberg tells me you are suffering from a rare form of iron poisoning."

I nodded silently. He narrowed his eyes and looked at me for a few moments. "Take better care of yourself. Rumor has it that this extravaganza is going to be the best in years."

I tried to smile but my stomach was starting to cramp again. I braced for a huge rumble and wished Mr. Papernick away. He turned, and just then my stomach let loose with a massive growl. A growl begging for food. Even a piece of broccoloaf. I prayed Mr. Papernick was out of earshot. But he turned around and gave me a shocked look.

"Must be some virus!"

I clutched my poor, empty stomach and tried to disappear under my desk.

After a long day of grumbles and rumbles—and coughs and sneezes—Hil, Sludge, and I headed for rehearsals. Sludge and Hil were busy discussing how to see if our plan had worked.

"I think the easiest way is to ask him to list the causes of World War I," said Hil. "If he can't do it, the plan has worked. If not, on to the next one."

"I have a better idea," said Sludge. "Let's see if he can whip up one of his famous soufflés."

Hil laughed. "That might be a tastier idea, Sludge, but not an easier one."

"Let's have him dissect a frog," suggested Sludge.

"Too gross," said Hil. "Why not have him draw and label a map of the pre-war Eastern Bloc countries?"

I gathered up all my strength; it took all my energy to get their attention.

"What about play rehearsal?" I asked. "They're all going to hear my stomach!" Hil looked thoughtful. "Sludge, remember when you talked about understudying the role of Romeo?"

"Yeah, and you laughed at me," said Sludge, suddenly downcast.

"True," said Hil. "But did you ever ask Mr. Kagan?"

"Weeeell, no. But I had it all planned out. Late-night rehearsals by the fire with my Juliet. Whispering the elegant prose of Shakespeare in her delicate ear. Digging deep to express Romeo's deep sorrow at finding and losing his true love—"

"Whatever," said Hil, cutting him off. "Here's the plan. Sludge, you are going to tell Mr. Kagan you desperately want to understudy Romeo. Tell him that with such short notice, the best way to learn your mark is to be right up there with Michael. Then you can cover up any weird noises with some of those bullfrog coughs you perfected in Thatcher's class."

"Cool plan," replied Sludge, "but Kagan got Phil Keats to understudy."

"Don't worry about Phil," said Hil. "You just offer your services to Mr. Kagan."

"What am I going to do about kissing Genevieve?" I moaned.

Hil was too impressed with her quick thinking to

worry about my dreaded meeting of the lips. "Kissing is the least of your worries," she said. "Just bite the bullet and do it, Romeo."

Rocks Mudman, Sam Rampalsky, Herb Everett, and Bob—otherwise known as Benvolio, Mercutio, Paris, and Tybalt—were finishing up their battle scene as we entered the gym. It was their favorite scene in the play—of course, since Sam played the murdered Mercutio, it was his last scene in the play—and they had worked endlessly on their sword fight. Sam had also put in extra time perfecting his death.

"Fabulous! Just fabulous!" cried Mr. Kagan. "Sam, I didn't know you could die with such dignity. If only you could put the same effort into your book reports!"

Even Harold looked impressed. He called for the next scene. Hil headed straight for Phil Keats while Sludge made a beeline for Mr. Kagan. In no time, Phil joined Sludge and Mr. Kagan.

"Quick change," announced Mr. Kagan. "Arthur Sludinsky will now be understudying the role of Romeo."

Sludge took his place beside me onstage.

"How did you do that so quickly?" I asked.

"Easy. Hil offered to do Phil's history paper if he suddenly came down with strep throat. I, of course, was just in the middle of telling Kagan how inspiring the whole play was when Phil broke the bad news of his sudden illness. Yours truly was there to pick up the pieces!"

Sludge and I moved to the wings of the stage as the scene started. It was the final act of the play, when Romeo finds the supposedly dead Juliet. We walked out to the middle of the stage. With Sludge by my side, I opened the tomb of Juliet and then slew Paris. We walked toward Genevieve, who lay motionless in her casket. I was preparing to make my final passionate speech when she opened one eye slightly and saw Sludge.

"What is *he* doing here?" she hissed under her breath, still trying to look dead.

"He's my understudy," I whispered back.

"Well, he'd BETTER not get in the way of our kiss," she warned.

I mustered up the last of my dwindling energy. "Eyes, look your last! Arms, take your last embrace! And, lips, O you the doors of breath, seal with a righteous kiss…"

It was time. I saw Genevieve pucker up. I could smell watermelon-flavored lip gloss. Her lips waited for mine. Slowly I bent over her. Our mouths were just about to touch when—

My stomach let loose with the biggest roar in the history of the Grade Eight Thespian Extravaganza Extraordinaire.

Terrified, Genevieve bolted from her coffin.

"What on earth was that?" wondered Mr. Kagan.

"Must have been an earthquake," offered Sludge helpfully.

"I felt the ground shake!" said Sam, who was also no longer playing dead.

"I think that's enough for today," decided Mr. Kagan.

Genevieve quickly regained her composure and focus. "But, Mr. Kagan, Michael and I didn't get a chance to practice the *most important scene in the entire play*."

"We're done for now, Genevieve," said Mr. Kagan. "If you think you need some extra rehearsal, why not run through the scene with our assistant director?"

Yes!

The only person less interested in kissing Genevieve than me was Wormald! His face was painted with a little fear and a lot of disgust.

"Is that all right with you, Harold?" asked Mr. Kagan.

He didn't have a chance to answer. Genevieve was already dragging him into a private corner.

"Nice work, Michael," said Hil, laughing, as she joined me and Sludge. "Did you see Harold's terrified face when Genevieve offered him some gum? You know he's going to make you pay for it. But this was totally worth it!"

Not that I wasn't proud of myself, but we had bigger concerns at that moment.

"Let's test this thing. I'm starving!" I snapped at them.

"Hey, man. Chill," said Sludge.

We had decided that the final test would be the first scene in *Romeo and Juliet*. Hil could see that I was tired and cranky. She got right to it.

"Act 1, scene 1," said Hil. "Two households, both alike in dignity…"

She gave me the first line of the play and waited tensely.

"Concentrate," she told me.

I felt a familiar rumble in my stomach. But this time it wasn't the rumble of hunger. I saw a quick flash of light and felt a flip in my empty tummy. The words came tumbling out.

In fair Verona, where we lay our scene,

From ancient grudge break to new mutiny,

Where civil blood makes civil hands unclean…

"I can't believe it," mumbled Sludge.

From forth the fatal loins of these two foes
A pair of star-cross'd lovers take their life—
"Enough! Enough!" he finally cried.

We sat together in stunned silence. Hil took a sandwich out of her backpack and handed it over. The plan hadn't worked; it was time to eat. But after days and days of fasting, suddenly I wasn't hungry.

Reality set in. I was going to be wired forever. Cursed as a genius for the rest of my life. Relegated to the lead of every play; top of the class; an over-achiever.

It wasn't fair.

Slowly I ate Hil's tuna sandwich. It was good—although a few capers or calamata olives would have added more flavor.

Sludge tried to put on a brave face. "If we put our heads together, I'm sure we can come up with a few more ideas."

I kept eating. Hil nodded her head halfheartedly. But Sludge wasn't giving up. "Come on, you guys. I can't believe you're throwing in the towel now! So maybe this idea and the last one didn't work. Big deal! We've got a lot more great ideas inside of us. Hey, maybe even the chip can come up with one or two!"

He grabbed a notebook and pencil from his bag. "Mike, if you give up now, you'll be the lead of every play in high school. Imagine having to kiss Genevieve for four more years!"

It was enough to make me stop eating! Hil even managed a smile. We started on a new list.

CHAPTER EIGHTEEN

Chaos on the Coaster

THE WEEKS LEADING UP to the extravaganza were a blur. Practices were mixed in with some schemes to get rid of the chip that got more and more crazy. Hil and Sludge did their best to keep an eye on Harold and his henchmen while I prepared for the play. I tried my best to keep Harold's rat-fink plots out of my mind. But sometimes it was hard.

"I found a disk in Harold's briefcase—a PowerPoint presentation called *Ten Easy Ways to Impeach Your President*," Hil told Sludge, thinking I couldn't hear.

"You think that's bad," replied Sludge. "I saw Harold in the computer lab printing business cards."

"Weird for an eighth grader to need business cards," agreed Hil.

"Yeah, but that's not the weirdest part. They said Harold Wormald, co-captain of the Mathlete squad, editor of *Hooray for History!*, president of J.R. Wilcott Middle School!"

"He's got something big up his sleeve," warned Hil.

⎯⎯⎯

The hectic pace was starting to take a toll. "We never see you anymore," complained my father one morning.

"Once the play is over, I'll cook you a meal you'll never forget," I promised my family.

It wasn't the play that was taking up my time today. After detention, Sludge and I ran to the art studio, where Hil and a bunch of other kids were putting the finishing touches on the sets. They looked fantastic. I made my way around the room, admiring all the hard work that had finally come together.

"Great stuff!" I told Louise Wu.

"Thanks. We've been working day and night," she replied proudly.

"Hey, Mike! Come check out the balcony," said Joe Jacobs.

A large wooden balcony was being sanded down in the back of the room.

"Awesome!" I said.

"It took us thirteen periods of shop," he confided. "Since the balcony scene is the most famous in the play, we thought you guys needed something special."

"It really does look terrific," I told him as I headed off with Hil and Sludge.

"What number are we at?" I asked them as we boarded the local bus.

"Only number five," replied Hil.

"And remind me. What's number five?"

"It's a goodie," assured Hil.

"Better than Sludge holding me upside down by the ankles, trying to shake the chip out of me?" That was number three on their list.

"Hey, I was gentle with you!" said Sludge.

"It's better than that," said Hil.

Half an hour later, we got off the bus. We were standing in front of Seabreeze Amusement Park. Now I remembered number five on the list.

The double-dipping, super-looping Firebrand roller coaster!

Sludge was positive this plan was going to work. He was so positive, he paid for our tickets to get into the park.

"A small price to pay to be rid of the chip once and for all," he said.

According to Sludge, the plan was simple. "Way less technical than the other plans. The chip needs a little more juice to get it moving, 'cause it's not moving on its own, if you know what I mean. You ride the Firebrand, and when the coaster turns upside down, you open your mouth. The chip should fall right out."

On most days, I would be thrilled to ride the Firebrand, but with the play just around the corner, I didn't have a lot of time to waste.

"How is this plan any different from you turning me upside down and shaking me?"

"Force. Much more force at work here, man," explained Sludge.

We headed for the waiting cars. Hil offered to sit with me, leaving Sludge to sit in the car behind us.

Suddenly, two thick arms grabbed my shoulders and pushed me forward into a different car. A big beefy hand covered my mouth so I couldn't yell for help. Seconds later I found myself sandwiched between Leon and Fletcher. I couldn't budge. The roller coaster slowly started up the hill.

I was trapped!

Craning my neck, I saw Hil and Sludge helplessly waving a few cars behind. Before I had a chance to ask Leon and Fletcher what the deal was, their fearless leader popped up in the car behind us. I should have known!

"There's nowhere to hide, Wise. I've got you right where I want you," he started.

When it came to writing evil speeches, Harold needed new material. But I had no choice but to listen.

"We've spent hours trying to figure out your secret to J.R. Wilcott domination. You led us to believe that your new brainpower came from drinking massive amounts of coffee. Not true! Then we studied the effects of broccoloaf on the retention of seventeen languages. Nothing! Staying up all night watching movies and studying their impact on our math skills. Nil! Extreme dieting leading to an improved saxophone performance. Nada! I have the detailed notes on my PC to prove it!"

As we climbed higher and higher, he got angrier and angrier. "You think you can fool me? Make me run lines with Genevieve so I miss valuable studying time? Force me to kiss her so I get distracted from my job as assistant director? I am the smartest guy in the whole school. I've got you all figured out, Wise, and I'm ready to bring you down. I'm giving you one final chance. Step down as school president and I'll forgo my plan to destroy you. It's an easy choice, Wise. Step aside and I'll let you finish the school year in peace." He sat back with a satisfied grin on his sneaky face.

Before I could answer him, we hit the famous Firebrand loops.

The coaster zoomed down the hill, through one queasy upside-down loop, and then through another curly loop. After one more giant loop-de-loop, we pulled back into the station.

"We're not leaving until I get your answer!" shouted Harold.

I could play this game, too. Plus, I needed some time to think. So we started up the hill for another turn on the Firebrand. Then another. And another.

Five roller coaster rides later, Leon was turning various shades of green. He lurched to a nearby bench. Fletcher had his head in a garbage can. Even I felt a little shaky.

Only Harold was fine. He was still demanding my answer.

"Quit and save your self-respect, Wise."

I couldn't see Hil and Sludge anywhere. But I had to make this decision on my own, anyway. Harold claimed to have me figured out, but he had yet to mention the computer chip. I decided to gamble on his knowledge.

"It's not happening, you rat-fink worm," I told him. "You'd better find some other way to bring me down, because I am ending the year as J.R. Wilcott's president."

Harold's face went a shade of purple I'd never seen. Could steam really come from human ears? He was so angry that he could barely blurt the words.

"You'll be sorry!"

I was worried, all right. But with Leon joining Fletcher at the wastebasket, I knew I had time for a quick getaway.

CHAPTER NINETEEN

Last Chance

"FINAL DRESS REHEARSAL!" bellowed Mr. Kagan. "Everyone, take your places. We are going to run through the entire play without stopping. Just like it's really show time! If anyone forgets a line, just keep going. Often the audience won't notice."

The sets were all in place. Joe's shop class had painted the balcony mahogany and added a white trim. Fully costumed, we all went to our marks. From the side, Hil gave me a nod. She was positive that Harold would strike at the play because he knew it meant so much to me, but she was confident that she could keep an eye on him. Bob and Sam jostled playfully with their shiny swords, also courtesy of Joe and his shopmates. They had created two foils that looked sharp enough to slice a watermelon in half, but were actually plastic.

"I've seen Bob play basketball and he's not always so sure on his feet," explained Joe. "This

126

way, if he stumbles, Sam won't lose his left arm."

Genevieve stood in the corner, touching up her lipstick. Even though I still had no interest in kissing her, she looked pretty hot. Her hair was pinned up on her head, with curls around her face. Her mother had sewn a blue dress for her, and she had matching flowers in her hair. She looked like the perfect Juliet—with the exception of her red-tipped nose.

"Just the sniffles," she told me, blowing delicately into a tissue. "Nothing to worry about. I've taken a cold tablet and will be fine for opening night."

Her cold didn't affect today's performance. She knew her lines by heart and didn't miss a mark in the early scenes. Aside from a few flubs from Rocks, everyone was just fine. Even Bob had somehow managed to learn his part. His fight scenes went much more smooth now that he didn't have to look offstage for cues. Mr. Kagan stood in front of the stage waving happily, silently mouthing our lines with us. It was perfect.

Genevieve peered soulfully into my eyes. "Ay, pilgrim, lips that they must use in prayer." And she leaned in to kiss me.

I quickly turned my head so she caught the corner of my ear.

"Your cold," I explained to her. "I don't want to get sick the night before the play."

"Fine." She frowned. "But no excuses tomorrow night. For the good of the extravaganza, you are going to kiss me. We're doing *Romeo and Juliet* because of you, so the least you can do is give a *full* performance come show time."

She was right. I had run out of time and excuses. Friday night, in front of the whole school, I would have to kiss Genevieve. And no doubt the other kids would get a big laugh watching their school president—the guy who'd gotten the cafeteria to switch from pizza to broccoloaf—fumble it like a first-timer.

We finished the rest of the rehearsal without any hitches. Mr. Kagan was sure this was going to be the best extravaganza ever. "I want everyone to go straight home and rest those precious voices! Hot tea and lemon before bed for everyone. Genevieve, be sure to keep yourself hydrated so your cold doesn't get any worse."

Hil and Sludge didn't come over that night. It was late by the time practice ended and we had all promised Mr. Kagan we would go home, do a few vocal exercises, and relax. Mom brought me tea and honey as I read in bed. I had found a tattered copy of Shakespeare's *Antony and Cleopatra*. It was a pretty good story—though I had no intention of being

Antony to Genevieve's Cleopatra. Mom sat beside me as I sipped my tea.

"Look at you!" she said. "Reading Shakespeare in your spare time."

"His romantic tragedies are pretty good," I admitted. "But I think I'm ready for some of the histories, where it gets real bloody."

"Shakespeare," repeated Mom. "In his spare time." She left the room shaking her head.

———

The day of the play was a whirlwind. I snuck downstairs at the crack of dawn, and Hil and Sludge came over for plans, six, seven, and eight. Show time was just around the corner so we had to act fast. Not only were we running out of time, we were also running out of ideas. The schemes were getting sillier and sillier. Hil and Sludge were desperate. They spent most of the time arguing over which of the plans was the dumbest. I was losing confidence in their ideas. But I felt strangely calm. Maybe life as a genius wouldn't be so terrible after all.

Hil glared at Sludge. "Plan six, even though Sludge thinks it's lame," she said angrily.

"It *is* lame!" Sludge shot back. "Where are we going to dig up a hypnotist in the next couple of minutes?"

"A hypnotist?" I repeated.

"Yes, a hypnotist," she said. "I've been doing some thinking about this. A computer needs memory to operate, right? It won't work if it doesn't have enough. So I did some research, and we're going to hypnotize you and make you lose all your memories." She corrected herself. "*I'm* going to hypnotize you and make you lose all of your memories."

"If I have no memory, how will I be able to remember my lines for the play?" I asked.

"We're running out of time. We'll worry about that later," she said brusquely. "Sit in the chair in front of me and keep your eyes on the watch.

"You are getting very, very sleepy," she said as she swung the watch on its chain. "Soon you will do exactly what I say."

Twenty minutes later, Hil was still swinging the watch, assuring me that I was getting very, very sleepy. Actually, I was getting very, very cross-eyed. I couldn't take any more.

"I'm sorry, Hil, but it's not working and we're running out of time. What's number seven on the list of plans?"

"Have you ever heard of anyone playing *Revenge of the Swamp Suckers* on an overheated computer?" she asked. "Probably not, because overheated computers are useless—they won't work. For this plan we'll need a sauna and we'll need to get it up to around 170 degrees."

"We don't know anyone with a sauna," I reminded her.

"Well, what about a really hot shower?" She was desperate.

It was time for their final plan. Sludge opened his backpack and pulled out a carton of eggs, a jar of mayonnaise, a bottle of cod-liver oil, Tabasco sauce, anchovy paste, a carton of sour milk, and a block of moldy cheese. Grabbing a large bowl from the kitchen cupboard, he set to work. First he cracked three eggs into the bowl. But instead of throwing the shells in the garbage, he crumpled them into crumbs and dropped them in as well. Next came the mayonnaise. He added a large splash of cod-liver oil, a smidgen of anchovy paste, and a dollop of Tabasco.

"Don't breathe in," he advised as he opened the sour milk and poured a generous cup into the mix.

Finally, he garnished the concoction with a smattering of crumbled, moldy cheese. "Stilton, the highest quality blue cheese," he told us. He handed me a spoon. "Dig in, dude."

"You actually think I am going to eat this?" I asked him incredulously. "No way! No chance!"

"But, Mikey, it's guaranteed to make you lose your last meal. First, you'll break out in the sweats, then you'll see spots, then you'll have a massive pain in your large intestine, and presto—everything you've eaten for the last forty-eight hours, plus the chip, will be on the floor."

"That's disgusting, Sludge!" complained Hil.

"How do you know it's going to work?" I asked him.

"I told you, man. It's guaranteed to work. I've seen it work with my own two eyes."

Slowly I took the spoon, dipped it into the concoction, and lifted it to my lips.

"I can't watch," moaned Hil, leaving the room.

The spoon was almost touching my lips.

Sludge covered his eyes with his hands.

I caught a whiff of the mixture... And dropped the spoon.

"I'm sorry, but I can't do it. You can uncover your eyes.

"I just can't," I explained to them. "It's not so much eating this disgusting mix as the possibility of getting sick on stage. The cast and crew have worked too hard to have me ruin it by barfing up my dinner in act 2. Plus, Genevieve would kill me!"

Sludge didn't seem so disappointed. "I suppose it was a bit extreme," he admitted.

We were all out of ideas. Hil looked glum. Sludge seemed upset with himself. It was up to me to cheer them up.

"Both of you, stop frowning! Sure, our plans didn't work, but we've got some big stuff ahead of ourselves tonight. We might not like the way we got stuck with this year's play, but we can all agree that this could be the best extravaganza ever! It's going to be a great play tonight, and we're all part of it. Hil, you're in charge of all the ushers. Sludge, you're the most important understudy. And in case anyone hasn't heard, I'm Romeo!"

"You'll be terrific," said Hil sincerely.

"Yeah, break a leg tonight," said Sludge warmly, patting me on the back. "Although if you do break a leg, I'll have to go on as your understudy!"

CHAPTER TWENTY

Showtime!

PEOPLE RUSHED INTO THE AUDITORIUM to get a good seat. I peeked through the curtain from backstage and saw Mom, Dad, and Howard sitting in the third row. Behind me, things were crazy. Hil was doing her best to keep an eye on Harold while handing out programs. Mr. Kagan was doing his best to calm everyone down. He put his arm around Rocks Mudman's shoulders. Rocks looked like he had just seen a ghost. Mr. Kagan must have been holding him up because Rocks's knees were clacking together and his legs were shaking like Jell-O.

"You'll be fine," assured Mr. Kagan in a soothing voice.

Rocks looked unconvinced. "What if I forget my lines like I did at the dress rehearsal? My lines—I can't remember *any* of them right now!" He was starting to get hysterical.

"You'll be fine," repeated Mr. Kagan calmly.

"You're the best Benvolio we have. And if you forget your lines, I'll be standing in the wings to help. But I doubt I'll have to, Rocks."

"Yeah, your adrenaline will really kick in when the spotlight starts to shine on you," said Harold, casually strolling by.

"Spotlight? What spotlight?" cried Rocks. He rushed off to find the nearest wastebasket. Behind me I heard delicate sneezes. It was Genevieve, red-eyed and runny-nosed. The cold medicine hadn't done its job.

"Are you going to be all right tonight?" I asked her. Losing Rocks to the wastebasket was one thing, but Genevieve was the soul of the play.

"Fear not, dear Romeo. A little virus is not going to stand in the way of my extravaganza debut," she declared. The cold had made her voice drop an octave. It made her sound more dramatic.

"I've spent the last two years in the chorus. I'm not going to let a cold get in the way of my—," she paused to sneeze, "—shining moment. We've all worked so hard and tonight we'll be able to show everyone. This is going to be the best extravaganza ever!" She grabbed a wad of tissues, from her pocket and gave her nose a long, hard blow.

"You're right," I said admiringly. Maybe kissing

Genevieve in front of everyone wouldn't be the worst thing in the world.

Especially if it made this year's extravaganza the best ever.

The rest of the cast was desperately trying to control their nerves. Rocks was slumped in a corner with the wastebasket by his side. Sam sat beside him, offering encouragement. In the opposite corner, Andrea had a needle and thread, and her fingers worked furiously.

"Bob accidentally stepped on the train of Louise's gown," she explained as she mended the tear.

Nearby, Bob stood straight and tall, without moving a muscle.

"Mr. Kagan told me to pretend I'm an iceberg. Said it's a relaxation technique that famous stage actors use before showtime," he mumbled, trying not to move his lips. It was a brilliant idea. It kept him from stepping on anyone else's costume.

Sludge sat on a bench quietly playing solitaire. Being an understudy meant that he wasn't going to get much action on stage tonight. Plus, with Hil distributing programs, Sludge wanted to keep an eye on Harold and his goons. Earlier, he had caught Leon and Fletcher painting green polka dots on Joe Jacobs's mahogany balcony. "If that's the best that rat fink's got," said Sludge, "we're in the clear."

Hil stopped by to grab more programs. "It's packed out there!" She looked around. "Is that Rocks with his head in the garbage can? Why is Bob looking so stiff?"

"Opening-night jitters," I said.

"Are you nervous?" she asked.

I wasn't. Not even about kissing Genevieve. I knew my lines, but in case I suddenly had a Rocks-like attack of nerves, the chip would be there to bail me out.

Mr. Kagan gathered us together for some words of encouragement. He could sense the fear. "Let's start with a quiet moment. Take a deep breath and try to focus."

We stood in silence, except for the occasional *honk* from Genevieve as she blew her nose.

Mr. Kagan pulled us close for a final word. "In a few minutes, it'll be curtain time. We've all put a lot of hard work into this project. It's time to show J.R. Wilcott the best ever Grade Eight Thespian Extravaganza Extraordinaire."

With a final round of high-fives, we took our marks. The curtain went up and the spotlight shone on center stage. Showtime! The chorus took their place. There was no turning back now! They spoke loudly and clearly:

Two households, both alike in dignity,
In fair Verona, where we lay our scene,
From ancient grudge break to new mutiny,
Where civil blood makes civil hands unclean.

"Act 1, scene 1," whispered Mr. Kagan.

Jim Rodgers and Sarah Henley took their spots on the stage. After a few lines, Sean Simmons and Emily Belmont joined them. Rocks stood in the wings, waiting nervously. His cue was when Jim and Sarah lifted their swords to do battle. His face was shiny with sweat. He kept wiping his clammy hands on his pants.

"Draw, if you be men!" bellowed Jim. He began to joust with Sarah.

"Rocks, you're on," whispered Mr. Kagan.

But Rocks didn't move. Mr. Kagan gave him one last pat on the back for support and gave him a shove—Rocks was suddenly center stage. For the first time I was nervous. Was Rocks going to come through? He looked terrified.

"Part fools," he mumbled meekly. Gaining a little confidence, he added, "Put up your swords; you know not what you do."

Bob took his cue as Tybalt. "What, art thou drawn among these heartless hinds? Turn thee, Benvolio, look upon thy death."

"I do but keep the peace; put up thy sword, or manage it to part these men with me," said Rocks loudly and clearly. He seemed surprised at the force of his own voice. His face broke out into a huge grin.

Offstage, Mr. Kagan let out a sigh of relief. Rocks was on track and the cast was doing a fabulous job. Lord and Lady Montague joined the scene. It was time for my entrance. Nervous energy mixed with plain old excitement flushed through my body. I walked what I hoped was elegantly onstage. "Good-morrow, cousin," Rocks said to me.

"Is the day so young?" I replied confidently. "Was that my father that went hence so fast?"

Looking out into the audience, I tried to project my voice just as Mr. Kagan had shown me. I moved my arms up and down with dramatic flourishes.

This was fun!

As Benvolio and Romeo, Rocks and I bantered back and forth. "To merit bliss by making me despair," I moaned dramatically, putting my hands over my heart. "She hath forsworn to love, and in that vow do I live dead that live to tell it now."

I didn't want the scene to end. Mr. Kagan was right: my adrenaline was pumping. It was electric, and I loved it! I wanted to stay onstage and recite everyone's lines.

Eventually Rocks and I exited the stage. We high-fived the second we were out of the audience's view.

"Awesome! Just awesome!" he crowed.

It really was! The night was speeding by. Harold and his empty threats were nowhere in sight. Before long, it was time for Genevieve and me to share our first scene together. I saw her pop a mint into her mouth.

Our kiss! In all the excitement, I had forgotten about the kiss.

I waited for the familiar combination of embarrassment and dread to wash over me. I waited and waited until Genevieve had finished two and a half mints—until it was almost time to go on stage. To my amazement, the feeling of dread was replaced by one of honor.

I was going to give Genevieve such a passionate kiss that it would have made William Shakespeare himself proud. The cast and crew deserved it.

Though the audience couldn't see it, both of Genevieve's sleeves were stuffed with soggy tissue. She made a quick dash to her gym bag to grab a fresh tissue. She returned with her face buried in her tissue-covered hands. I noticed how her long blue dress made her look so tall. We walked onstage. Slightly in front of me, Genevieve wobbled as she walked. High heels and cold medicine were a bad combination. She teetered and tottered as she took her place, her back against mine.

It was the scene where we fall instantly and madly in love with each other. We were supposed to turn around slowly and our eyes would meet as I uttered my lines, "If I profane with my unworthiest hand this holy shrine, the gentle fine is this: my lips, two blushing pilgrims, ready stand to smooth that rough touch with a tender kiss." Genevieve was turning around very slowly. Her head was bowed to the floor. I could have sworn that she had her hair in a curly updo, but now her long blond hair covered her face. She had decided to play the scene very shy.

"A tender kiss," I repeated, even though it wasn't in the script.

Slowly, Juliet looked up into my eyes. I guessed that deep down she was as embarrassed as I was. Her earlier attempts to practice the scene must have just been a cover.

Our eyes met for our first kiss, and I realized...

It was Fletcher.

Somehow, between scenes, my Juliet had been replaced by this hulking lug of a Juliet! Harold stood in the wings, doubled over in evil laughter. His plan to bring me down was being played out in front of the whole school.

Desperately I caught his eye. As Fletcher puckered up his lips for a kiss, Harold laughed harder.

Actually, with his big blue eyes and rosy cheeks, Fletcher made a fine-looking Juliet. But we needed to find *my* Juliet... And quickly!

Offstage, Hil grabbed Harold by the collar. As she tried to find out what had happened to Genevieve, I stalled for time. I performed my favorite soliloquy from *Antony and Cleopatra.* The audience looked impressed.

I recited my lines in Spanish, Polish, Danish, and Swahili. Fletcher looked impressed.

Just when I was about to offer the recipe for Hungarian crêpes, my true Juliet burst onto the stage. With a giant shove, she pushed Fletcher offstage. A quick nose-blow, and she was ready for our much-anticipated kiss.

Coming close, she whispered, "Harold locked me in the broom closet!"

Taking a deep breath, I said my line, "A tender kiss," for the third and final time and leaned in. Genevieve looked shocked at my eagerness. She shouldn't have been—she was a much better choice than Fletcher.

I closed my eyes and leaned in to place a romantic kiss on her lips. *Long live the Grade Eight Thespian Extravaganza Extraordinaire*, I thought, as our lips met.

The whole school watched intently. A second later it was over. We finished the scene and exited the stage.

"Michael! What a fabulous kiss," Genevieve purred between sneezes. "Everything I had expected and so much more." She touched her lips to make sure they were still there.

Hil was instantly at my side. "I can't believe that worm pulled one over on us! He's the one locked in the broom closet now."

My lips were tingling strangely from the kiss.

Hil continued. "He thought he was so smart, but he caved the moment I demanded to know where he had hidden Juliet. He thinks he's so evil, but he folded like a house of cards when I got through with him." She shadow-boxed, jabbing punches as she talked.

I wasn't paying much attention—I wasn't feeling so hot anymore. I let out a massive belch. My stomach was aching. First it was just mild pains, like I had eaten some bad salami. But now it was a burning sensation—like a surging force of cramps eating away at my stomach.

Salami had never been this bad!

I crouched close to the floor, holding my stomach, praying for the pain to go away. I was Romeo! I had a play to perform!

"Are you okay?" asked Genevieve. "Did the passion of our kiss wipe you out?"

I had to go back on stage for the next scene. Gingerly, I made my way out. I wasn't nervous, but my legs were shaking and my shoulders were trembling. I felt as though I had lost control of my body. It was my line. I tried to pull myself together.

"CanIgoforwardwhenmyheartishereturnbackdull earthandfindthycenterout."

The words came out of my mouth in a mumbled jumble.

I tried again but the words surged out, impossible to understand.

"CanIgoforwardwhenmyheartishereturnbackdull earthandfindthycenterout."

Confused, I looked offstage to Mr. Kagan. He motioned to his stomach and raised his arms. He thought I was nervous. He wanted me to take a deep breath and relax. I took his suggestion. Taking a deep breath, I tried it once more.

"C-c-c-c...can, uh, I g-g-g-go f-f-for-ward w-when m-m-m-my h-h-hear-t-t-t i-sss h-h-h-er-r-r-e. T-t-t-turr-n b-baa-ck d-duull earrrth a-n-d f-f-f-ind th-y cennter o-uuu-t," I sputtered.

I knew the words, but I couldn't get them out of my mouth. It was as though my brain and mouth were no longer communicating with each other. Thankfully the scene was short. I rushed offstage.

"What's wrong with you?" asked Genevieve.

My stomach felt like it was melting, but I said nothing. Mr. Kagan still assumed it was an attack of nerves. "Just relax. Try and have fun out there," he advised.

"Act 2, scene 2!" he called out.

It was the most important scene in the play. Romeo declares his love to Juliet as she stands on Joe Jacobs's polka-dotted mahogany balcony. My stomach still burned. How was I going to make it through the rest of the play in such pain? I took a few more deep breaths.

Suddenly it stopped. The burning pain was gone. So was the melting sensation. My mouth felt fine. My knees and shoulders stopped shaking. Everything was back to normal.

In fact, I felt lighter on my feet than I had in months! Maybe it *was* just a brutal attack of nerves.

Confidently, I strolled to center stage, looked out into the audience, and prepared to deliver my pivotal lines. It was my shining moment in the extravaganza—the dramatic highlight of the play. My lines would move the audience to tears, making them yearn for a past love. My elegant reading would set the audience up for the heartbreak of the final scene. My lines would…

My lines… My lines…

My lines!

Suddenly, I couldn't remember any of my lines. I looked around the stage, hoping it was actually someone else's cue, but the spotlight shone in my eyes. It was definitely my line…and I had no idea what it was! All I could do was stand in front of the school, silent, dumbfounded. The heat from the spotlight was making me sweat.

The silent seconds felt like minutes. Soon it *was* minutes.

Slow,

silent,

painful

minutes.

I was desperate for my lines. But not one word was coming to me. Because of the chip I knew the whole play—not just my lines but Bob's, Rocks's, Sam's, and Genevieve's, too.

WHY COULDN'T I REMEMBER MY LINES? The spotlight still shone in my eyes. Someone in the audience began to cough. My knees began to knock.

Desperate, I turned to Mr. Kagan for help. He saw

the fear in my eyes. *But soft what light through yonder window breaks*, he mouthed.

I couldn't make out what he was saying.

"But soft what light through yonder window breaks," he whispered, hoping to spark my memory.

I repeated the words helplessly.

"It is the east, and Juliet is the sun," whispered Mr. Kagan.

He looked worried. And for good reason. The words had deserted me—not even any spluttering or stuttering—and they weren't coming back, no matter how many lines Mr. Kagan fed me. Genevieve, looking down from the balcony, didn't know what to do.

Neither did I. I had a speech to give—a famous speech—but I couldn't remember the words.

I looked out into the audience. Thankfully, I couldn't make out any faces. But I knew they could see the sweat dripping off mine.

"I don't know," I finally told them, still standing in the glare of the spotlight. "I don't know my lines."

They stared at me in silence. Even the coughing had stopped.

"I'm sorry," I added weakly.

The room was silent.

Suddenly, I heard someone clapping from the

back of the room. Then a few other hands joined in. A couple of hoots soon followed. Then some rowdy hollers. People began to get out of their chairs and applaud wildly. I had no idea what was going on. I looked to the side of the stage, and my classmates were jumping up and down with joy!

"We got our man back!" yelled Albert Hogan joyfully.

"It took long enough," said Smashmouth Garello, hugging Andrea Hackenpack. "But I knew that Mike would come through!"

"Maybe he's not such a showoff after all," pondered Marty Jenkins.

The noise was incredible. Kids were standing on their seats, screaming at the top of their lungs in pure joy. A few parents even joined in the applause. My parents looked confused, but they stood up and clapped when the crowd began to chant my name. I held up my arms, shrugged, and took a bow.

The crowd went wild.

I blew a kiss to the audience. The room went even wilder.

And then I was no longer alone on stage. I turned around to see Sludge, dressed in purple tights with a purple plume sticking elegantly out of his hat. He doffed his cap and everyone went crazy.

"But soft! What light through yonder window breaks? It is the east and Juliet is the sun. Arise, fair sun, and kill the envious moon," he said to the audience, giving me a wink.

Giving him a quick bow, I turned the stage over to my understudy.

Hil and Mr. Kagan were waiting backstage. Kagan got to me first.

"What happened out there?" He sounded more concerned than angry.

"I don't know," I answered. "One minute I was fine and the next I was a mess. I kissed Genevieve, and then suddenly I forgot all of my lines." I felt a little tickle in my throat. "I think I must be coming down with her virus."

Her virus! Hil and I looked at each other in surprise.

"I can't believe we didn't think of that ourselves," she said in disbelief. "Genevieve's cold—a cold is a virus! And viruses destroy computer chips. When you kissed Genevieve, you caught her virus, which instantly destroyed the chip and caused you to forget all your lines!"

"And the whole time we were riding upside-down roller coasters!" I said, laughing.

"That wasn't my idea," said Hil, giggling. "It was pure, one hundred percent Sludge!"

Sludge! In all of the excitement, we had forgotten he was on stage. Quickly, we moved to the wings to get a look at him.

"She speaks. O, speak again, bright angel!" he said, gazing lovingly into Juliet's eyes.

"He's fabulous," whispered Hil.

And he was. The audience was captivated. Mr. Kagan was beaming. Sludge was a shoo-in for the lead next year.

"Hey," I said quietly to Hil. "Want to come over tomorrow night for a little celebration dinner? I found a great recipe for tiramisu and I'd love to try it out. I'll ask Sludge, too."

"I think you've lost all your cooking skills," said Hil.

"I did, but I didn't lose my appetite! I'll probably have to pay a little more attention to the recipe now, but I bet I can pull it off."

"I think I'm talking to Michael 2.0," said Hil, smiling.

I smiled back at her. "Actually, I have a great idea for next year's Grade Nine Fabulous Festival! Shakespeare's *Hamlet* is a great story about revenge. It's got murder, graveyards, and ghosts. Best of all, there's no kissing!"

The thought of smooching brought our attention back to Sludge. Explaining the tortured mind of poor

Hamlet would have to wait for later. Instead we watched our friend light up the stage.

"You know, he gets to kiss Juliet soon," I said.

"I'm sure he's looking forward to that," replied Hil.

"As long as it's not Fletcher!"

Sure enough, Sludge turned to us, winked, and popped a mint into his mouth.